STRONGER

THE UNIT
BOOK TWO

BESTSELLING AUTHOR
SARAH GREYSON

STRONGER

SARAH GREYSON

CONTENTS

STRONGER

CHAPTER ONE

Lola was lost in her own world as she moved her hips to the sensuous Latino beat. Alone, she attracted men, but on the dance floor, she was ruthless. She felt the man pressed up against her rear, although she never turned around to see what he looked like. She was there to dance. Some would consider her a tease; she would never go home with this man or any other man at the club. She never did. She just wanted to dance, to let herself go to the beat of the music.

She lifted her hands suggestively over her head and held them in the air while she gyrated her hips and danced to the carnal song. The ballad screamed sex, and many couples looked like they were having it right there on the dance floor. She moved against the man behind her and felt his hardness press against her. With the way she moved, it was hard to imagine at twenty years old she was still a virgin, but it had been ingrained in her to wait until she was married. Her first act of rebellion against her father should have been to have sex with as many people as possible, but she wanted to wait for the right man.

"I'm saving you!" Jessica shouted into her ear.

Lola opened her eyes for the first time during the song and saw her best friend standing before her on the dance floor.

"From what?" Lola asked with a smirk playing on her lips. *Oh, how she loved to tease.*

"Come on," Jessica responded, grabbing her hand and leading her off the dance floor. Lola felt the man groan against her but didn't turn around to look at him. She followed Jessica to the table where she found Samantha, aka "Sam," and Monica waiting with drinks in hand. Picking up her vodka-cranberry, she took a nice, long swallow. She needed a glass of water, or she would have a killer hangover in the morning.

"Excuse me. Can I get a water please?" Lola asked as the waitress passed. The waitress nodded and disappeared into the crowd. She couldn't wait to tell the girls about her lunch with Shelty. The snob desperately wanted to be part of their group, but no one wanted to add Shelty as a member. It was fine with the four of them. They were each down-to-earth, despite all growing up filthy rich. Lola's father was the CEO of a major airline company and had more money than she ever had to worry about, but he kept her under his thumb. He sheltered her from any dangers the real world possessed. She was treated like a princess kept under guard in her tower while God only knew what was happening in the real world. He wouldn't even allow her to watch the news for fear of corrupting his princess.

Sam's father inherited his money from his father; they were old money, and of the four, Sam was the most frugal. Shopping with Sam had always been a trip. She only went to the sale racks, even though she could afford to drop four grand on the latest handbag. Sam's frugalness was what Lola admired most about her. That and they shared the same dream: to escape from under their fathers' thumbs. To be free, independent women, ruled by no man. In her first act of freedom upon moving into the dorms at Harvard, Lola purchased a fake ID, which fooled even trained police officers. It was with that little treasure she was able to frequent all the Boston hotspots.

"Grant is good," Monica said, admiring her fake ID. She couldn't believe he had made it in under a week.

"That's why they are so expensive. He's the best," Lola replied. Changing the subject, Lola shouted to her three friends huddling at the table, "You'll never believe what that bitch Shelty did today."

"Why do you even hang out with her? Just ignore her like I do," Monica replied. "We all know what a spoiled little brat she can be." Monica took a sip of her Ketel vodka martini. She may be down to earth, but she never skimped when it came to her alcohol.

"We were sitting there, and she raised her voice and yelled to get the waitress's attention, like she owned the place. Everyone was disgusted at her obnoxiousness. She has no manners, I swear," Lola bellowed through the music. "Then she went on to order broiled boneless Mahi-Mahi with fresh lemon on the side. 'If I find a bone, I will send the whole entree back,'" Lola said, pinching her nose to create her best snooty impression of Shelty. "Her broccoli had to be done to perfection, a crisp green, or she would be sending it back. And, for an appetizer, she ordered a Zen Plate at $150. She is the most pretentious woman I have ever met. I will not be hanging out with her again, no matter what Daddy says," Lola huffed.

"You're much better off slumming it with us," Jessica said as a bright smile lit her face. Just because they were rich and privileged didn't give them the right to treat others the way Shelty did. They had good manners and actually cared about others' feelings.

"One more dance and then we'll call it a night. It's already after 1:00 a.m.," Lola begged her three friends at the table. One by one, they finished their drinks and followed Lola onto the dance floor. As they approached, several men did as well and asked for dances. They were incredibly good looking, and each of them grabbed a partner. Lola moved her body against the man's with her eyes closed, absorbing the beat. She felt his hands on her waist and noticed them creep higher until they were right under her breasts. She permitted it and kept on dancing. The backs of his hands were now brushing the underside of her breasts. He pulled her closer, and she could feel his breath against her neck as he buried his head into her long, golden blond hair that hung down to the middle of her back. She could feel the sweat drip down between her ample bosoms. Her killer curves were keeping her dance partner quite interested, making her feel confident and sexy.

All of a sudden, her eyes popped open as the hairs on the back of her neck started to prickle. Her body was covered in goose bumps. She could feel two holes burning into her. Someone, somewhere meant to do her harm. She could feel it. Frantically, she looked around trying to spot the danger. The club was crowded, preventing her from seeing who was staring at her. Turning, she thanked the man for the dance and tried to pull away, but his grip tightened on her and he wasn't letting go. She caught his eyes as dread crept up the back of her throat.

She had been so busy searching the crowd, she'd failed to notice the danger right in front of her. "With your killer body and looks, my finder's fee just tripled," the man said more to himself than to her. He held her deathly tight; she couldn't move, no matter how hard she struggled against him. "You're going to come with me, and you're going to be quiet about it, or my friend over there," he motioned, "will kill your three girlfriends," the man said, turning his eyes in the direction of his friend. Her eyes followed and locked onto the man in question. He smirked and waved at her. She stood frozen, watching as his gaze found Jessica.

The man held her tightly by the arm and pulled and pushed her through the crowd. She was too afraid to make a noise to notify security. If anything happened to Sam, Jessica, or Monica because of her, she would never forgive herself. She had always felt safe and secure in Boston and never felt threatened in Cambridge at Harvard University. Sure, most of the people who went there were rich, but she always felt safe. Boston had a good police presence, which dramatically increased after the bombing at the Boston Marathon.

She moved quietly beside the man. He was a quite attractive Latino man with a large frame and muscles visible through this button-down shirt, and at first she felt no warning bells go off when he approached her. That was always her tell; what her gut said about someone. She was rarely wrong. *He must be really good,* she thought as they moved their way past her friends. They were busy dancing and having fun. Terror gripped her as they slipped past them unnoticed and all hope of help was lost. They would surely go crazy at the end of the night when they couldn't find her. She only had her cell phone, debit card, and her fake ID. The man pushed open the door to the club and tightened his grip on her arm.

"Very good," he said to her with frightening sincerity. He patted her down and found her cell phone, ID, and debit card. *Great, now he was going to know her name, if he didn't already.*

What did he want from her? Perhaps he knew who she was and was planning to ransom her father. *What would happen to her now?* He forced her down the block to an alleyway where a dark blue cargo van was parked. He opened the side door and looked around. Pushing her inside quickly, he crawled in behind her, never letting go of her arm. When she was seated in the van, he pulled out rope and duct tape. With precision and speed, he had her hands tied together behind her and secured to a metal hook jutting up from the floor of the van before she had time to blink. Next, he taped her ankles together. Finally, he ripped a piece of duct tape and placed it over her mouth.

She sat in the back of the van, bound and gagged for several minutes. Her abductor shut the side door and got in the front passenger's seat. *They must be waiting for someone.* Another few agonizing minutes passed. All she could think about was praying to God his friend hadn't harmed her friends. She was strong; she would make it out of this. Tugging and pulling on her bonds was useless and only chafed her wrists. The fear was immense and overpowering. She didn't know who this man was or what was happening; she was terrified for her friends. Facing the back of the van, she heard the driver's side door open and felt the van shift as another man climbed inside.

"What do ya think?" the driver asked the passenger.

"At least ten, if not more. She's a knockout. If it is determined that she's a virgin? Twenty…easy," the passenger assured the driver. "Do I know how to pick 'em or what? All that long, blond hair, and she smells so good, like honeysuckle. Her body rocks! You can tell she takes care of herself. I felt her arms and her body; she definitely works out…a lot."

She could feel the bile rising in the back of her throat. The more the men talked, the worse it got. She couldn't get sick; she would choke to death. She did her best to choke the vomit back down. Sweat was trickling down her forehead, and it was getting harder to catch her breath. *Where were they taking her? What are they talking about?* It was at moments like this she wished to God her father hadn't sheltered her as much as he had. At least she knew her friends were safe. There was no way the driver had enough time to kill all three of her friends and make it to the van as quickly as he did.

The passenger crawled into the back of the van. Lola cowered. She wasn't sure what he planned on doing. He pulled out a syringe, gently moved the hair from the side of her neck, and pushed her head to the side. He plunged the needle into the carotid artery. As she faded into unconsciousness, her last thought was that she needed a plan.

CHAPTER
TWO

"You better slow down, or I'm gonna have to carry you outta here," Tony predicted as his friend nursed his fifth double scotch in less than three hours. "It's their wedding, man. Do you really want him worried about you all night?"

"He doesn't need to worry about me. I'm here to have a good time, dance with the bride, and show my support," Rob assured him, dismissing Tony's concern. Although the truth was, he was miserable, and seeing his best friend Michael so happy with Emma, the woman he saved instead of saving his Lizzie, only made him drink more. He had to become numb in order to support his friend. Hell, he had to become numb to stop the constant motion picture of her death looping through his mind. Although a year had passed, every day he lived with the pain of losing Lizzie. Every day, every minute, he heard her muffled groans and cries as the terrorist bastards raped her to death.

His mother kept telling him time heals all wounds. Well, time wasn't doing shit for him. He took as many jobs as Blackrain Security could provide. He hoped he would get shot in the line of duty and his misery would end. Twice he'd tried to kill himself since they found

Lizzie dead; both times his brothers had rescued him. He knew he was a coward, because only a coward would try and kill himself with pills and a bottle. If he were more of a man, he would put a gun to his head and get it over with. He tried many times, but could never pull the trigger. Visions of Lizzie always stopped him. He knew she would want him to be happy. She would want him to move on and forgive himself. Still, he had no idea how to do any of those things, so he drank until he couldn't remember who he was anymore. He drank until the movie stopped playing in his mind. He drank until he passed out.

"Earth to Rob. Rob. Are you alright?" Michael asked, standing in front of him. "I'm going to toss the garter now, and you need to be in that group of single men." Rob shot Michael a look that instantly silenced him. "Look, you see that hot blonde over by the bar? She's here alone. That's Emma's friend, Bethany. Why don't you talk to her? Maybe even dance with her? From what I've heard from Emma, she'll be interested. She likes your type," Michael coaxed, doing his best to try and pull Rob out of his funk.

"Maybe I should see if she would like to fuck; I mean dance." Rob coughed and rose unsteadily to his feet. He knew how to get Michael off his case. "One dance, but I'm not promising anything. I need another drink anyways," he said as he proceeded to swallow the gulp left in his tumbler. He had forgiven Michael, but he hadn't forgotten everything that inevitably lead to Lizzie's death. He stalked off towards Bethany, stopping and standing next to her at the bar.

"Can I buy you a drink?" he asked Bethany as a slow, sly grin appeared at the corner of his lips.

"Well, seeing as it's an open bar, I don't think you can buy me anything, but I will have a drink with you," Bethany said in her most flirtatious voice.

Even though Rob was entering the comfortably numb phase of his stupor, he noticed her flirting and decided why not. It had been a good month since he had gotten laid.

"You are a very beautiful woman. What are you doing here alone?"

"My date cancelled on me at the last minute. Not enough time to find a new one," Bethany said, flushing at the compliment. She batted her eyelashes at him. "I have no one to dance with."

"Would you care to dance?" Rob asked, turning on the charm.

"I would love to," she said, holding out her hand to him.

Rob took it, smiling as the DJ played a slow song. He led her to the dance floor, and she put her arms around his neck. He could admit she was a looker. He could use her to take his mind off things tonight and get his brothers to back off for a while. They always wanted to fix him. Didn't they realize there was no fixing his kind of broke?

In a daring move, Bethany pressed her breasts against his chest. He reciprocated by lowering his hands from her waist to her hips. She pressed closer, close enough for him to inhale her expensive perfume. She smelled nice. Yes, she would take his mind off of

Lizzie for the night. He moved in, nuzzling her neck. He felt nothing as he heard her breath catch in her throat. He knew he had her then. He moved his hands lower until they touched the top of her ass.

"Want to go back to your place?" Rob whispered into Bethany's ear. He knew he would have hell to pay with Emma and Michael for sleeping with her and then sneaking out of Bethany's house in the middle of the night. All he was after was a long, hard fuck—a way to release his pent-up energy. Masturbating wasn't even a possibility anymore. Every time he tried, the movie of Lizzie's death played in his head. The only way was to be with a woman, and there had been numerous ones over the course of the last six months. He couldn't very well go around beating people up to release his anger and frustration like he had once done to Michael. Now, his way, the woman got a good fuck, and he released his frustration on her in a way that had left several women begging for more.

Sometimes, he needed it once a month, other times, once a week. On rare occasions, two or three times a week. Because he was an attractive man, women were always throwing themselves at him. His dark hair was short and had the sexy, rumpled look. Like someone had just run her hands through it in a fit of passion. He had a chiseled jaw line and perfectly defined cheekbones. His body was cut and defined; anyone could see it through the way his button-down shirt stretched across his broad shoulders and pulled at his biceps. His hips narrowed, and he worked hard to maintain the V on both his front and his back. His slacks pulled across his thighs, showing off his muscular legs. But what brought the ladies to him was the triple threat: his gray eyes were haunted, mysterious; his lips were bowed and god-like; and his hands were masculine and calloused with close cut nails and veins popping out on the tops. He smiled at Bethany, throwing her a quirk which showed off his dimple in his left cheek. Panty. Dropping.

"We have to stay until they leave. If you still want to after that, I'm game," Bethany whispered back in his ear. When the dance was over, Rob extended his hand to her. Just because he was going to fuck her and leave her didn't mean he couldn't be a gentleman about it. She took his hand, and he led her to the bar. Once their drinks were filled, he led her back to his table. Michael approached with a leery look in his eyes. Rob noticed the way he glanced from Bethany's hand to his own resting together high up on Rob's thigh. Rob read the warning in Michael's eyes. Yep, Rob would have hell to pay for messing with Emma's best friend. But hey, she was here, and she was willing, and approaching her was Michael's suggestion in the first place. They were both consenting adults, and neither one needed their friends' approval.

"Rob, can I talk to you for a second?" Michael asked, motioning for Rob to follow. Once they got to a private corner, Michael continued. "I asked you to dance with her, not fuck her. Not with Bethany. She is Emma's best friend. You fucking her and leaving her will hurt her."

"I appreciate your concern, but I need this tonight. I'm happy for you and Emma, you know that, right? It's just so hard watching you two, knowing I will never have that again. She knows what I'm all about, and she's still game. We're both adults capable of making our own decisions. If she wants to take me back to her place, then I'm going to go," Rob informed his friend.

"Just make sure you explain your expectations before you leave with her. That way she knows exactly what she's getting into," Michael admonished Rob.

"Fine. If that's what it takes to make you happy, consider it done," Rob assured his friend, laying his hand on Michael's shoulder and giving it a squeeze. He didn't want to start any sort of trouble. He would do as his friend asked because he did care about Emma and, by extension, Bethany.

After watching the bride and groom cut the fragile cake covered in flowers and then delicately feed it to each other, Rob said his goodbyes and wished them a wonderful honeymoon in Aruba. If anyone deserved happiness, they did. He knew firsthand everything they went through in stopping the terrorist cell that had taken his Lizzie. He walked back to Bethany and asked if she was ready to leave.

"Let me grab my purse," she said, leaving him standing alone near the entrance. She returned anxiously, eager for what the night had in store. He reached for her hand and led her outside.

"I'll bring you back to get your car tomorrow," she offered. *Fuck, how was he going to sneak out of her bed now?* He would walk home. God knew he did plenty of walking as a former Green Beret.

STRONGER

CHAPTER
THREE

Lola's eyes felt heavy as she struggled to open them. She didn't know how long she had been unconscious, nor did she know where she was. She smelled a musty odor, like it had just rained, and wherever she was felt damp and moldy. She was lying on a lumpy mattress with her head on an even lumpier pillow, yet she still couldn't open her eyes. Then she heard it. At first it sounded far off in the distance, but the more she came to, the closer the voices sounded. They were the voices of females talking in another language. She recognized the French from the classes she'd taken in school. Then she exhaled as she heard English coming from someone near her.

"Hey. You awake?" the voice asked.

She was still too groggy to open her eyes or respond. She had to pull out of whatever lethargy the drug had caused. She never did drugs, not even prescription medicines. In the darkness, the memories came flooding back to her.

She was fourteen when she found her mother lying on the en suite floor, unresponsive to Lola's pleading. Dead. She'd known about the prescription medicines, but it wasn't until after the funeral that her father told her that her mom had abused them.

She remembered when her mother had hurt her back, and the doctor prescribed pain medication. Her initial injury healed, but she was never able to get off the medication and, apparently, because of their wealth, she was able to get whatever she wanted with a simple phone call. It came to light that her father knew all along about her addiction to pain medication and had even tried committing her mother three times to stays at a rehabilitation facility, the best money could buy. But it was no use; she was an addict.

When she found her lying on the floor, Lola raced to her side and dropped to her knees. Tears immediately streamed down her face as she shook her and pleaded with her to wake.

"Help! Help us!" she screamed. Eventually the staff heard her cries and came running into the bathroom. "Call 9-1-1," she cried. After what felt like forever, the ambulance finally arrived but pronounced her dead at the scene. Lola was never the same afterwards. All of her fond memories of her mother were stained by the vision of her lifeless body lying on that floor.

Drugs robbed her of a mother. Lola swore to herself she would never touch the stuff, and in her twenty years, she never had. She would suffer through headaches so she didn't have to take a pill. She was pissed at her mother for not being strong enough to get off drugs. Pissed her mom had left her when she needed her the most, at the tender age of fourteen.

Pissed she didn't care who found her, not even if it was her only child. She never had anyone to share stories of her first kiss with, never had anyone to share any of her success stories with. She had been robbed of her childhood on that very dark day.

Now she found herself drugged and in a foreign environment. Definitely not the Ritz Carlton. She was someplace dirty and uncomfortable, and from the sounds of it, she was with other women. *What did they want from her?* Maybe everyone here was being held for ransom.

She felt herself coming back and started to blink rapidly to clear the drug-induced sleep from her mind. What she saw shocked her, and she shrank back into the bumpy mattress. There was a stunning brunette standing over her asking her questions. She tried hard to make sense of her words.

"Êtes-vous d'accord?" the brunette asked.

"Qui êtes-vous?" Lola replied. "Parlez-vous Anglais?"

"Yes, a little," the brunette responded, shoulders slumping with relief that Lola was awake and alert.

"Where am I?"

"I not sure. We have no, how do you say, clue." The brunette girl spoke with a heavy French accent. "We sit here and wait for medicine and food."

"How long have I been here, asleep?" Lola asked the brunette as a beautiful redhead appeared and answered in perfect English.

"You have been here a while. You arrived when the sun was directly overhead, and now it's dark. We were worried when you didn't respond right away. Once we arrived, none of us stayed under as long as you did."

Lola looked around, and what she saw frightened her. She didn't know places like this even existed in America. She noticed a straw roof, which must leak when it rained, accounting for the moldy and musty smell. The walls were made of bamboo and were crawling with insects. The placed swarmed with them. She noticed a rather large bug crawling up her cot towards her. She waved her arms, screamed, and with one jump was immediately off of her cot and standing on the earth-packed floor. Upon further inspection, she noticed five cots in the small hut, including hers. There was a bucket in the corner of the room. "What's that?" She pointed to the bucket, but by the smell of urine and feces, she had a pretty good idea.

"That's the latrine," the French girl responded.

"We try to give each other privacy by turning our backs. But they only empty it once a night, so the smell is something you have to get used to," the English girl replied. Morbid curiosity pulled Lola closer to the bucket. Within a foot, she began to gag on the smell. Insects covered the contents of the bucket.

She'd gone from princess to prisoner in the span of a day.

"I'm Lola," she said, extending her hand to the other girls, showing her ingrained good manners. The French girl just looked at her outstretched hand, but the English girl grabbed it with her same hand and gently squeezed her fingers. "How long have you been here?"

"I have been keeping track in the dirt under my bed. I have been here nineteen days," the English girl responded. "I'm Alisha." She pointed to the redhead and said, "That's Cece. And over there is Dangani. She's African, but she can speak French and English." For the first time, Lola took in the African girl's features. She looked young, not much older than fourteen. Her body had not yet matured to that of a woman.

"How old is everyone?" Lola asked.

"I'm sixteen," Alisha responded. "Cece is seventeen, but Dangani is only thirteen. We try to look out for her. How old are you?"

"I'm twenty," Lola responded, trembling with fear as to what her captors' plans were. "You said they brought medicine. What kind?"

"They bring it three times a day. It makes the stay here more tolerable. Like you just don't care that you're here," Alisha said in a tone that communicated the helplessness of the situation.

"And if you don't take it?" Lola asked, dreading the answer.

"Then they shoot you full of something that makes you pass out. Trust me, you want the pill," young Alisha replied. How was Lola going to swallow a pill after she committed herself to never turning into her mother? She couldn't get hooked on anything that made her not care; she wouldn't be the brazen princess people had grown to love. That was if she was ever getting out of here.

"Have they ransomed your parents?" Lola asked hopefully, because her daddy would pay whatever he had to, to get his princess back.

"They don't talk to us. We're lucky if they grunt at us when it's time to eat. We have no idea why we're here. Although, a doctor did examine all of us, inside and out," Alisha warned. "On our second day here, a doctor came in and made me spread my legs. I don't know what they were looking for."

"Did it hurt?" Lola asked as her brows pulled together waiting for the answer.

"No, he was very gentle," Alisha responded.

Lola exhaled a breath she didn't know she was holding. "What about her? Dangani? Does she talk?" Lola pointed to the girl curled into the fetal position on her cot.

"Yeah, she talks. Her medicine has kicked in. That's how she gets when she takes it. Me, I am still able to talk; I just don't give a shit about anything, which is nice, ya know?" Alisha counseled.

"Me too," Cece concurred.

Just then the door opened and a tall, lanky Latino man with a pit-marked face entered the room.

"Glad to see you're finally awake," the man spoke in perfect English. "I was beginning to worry Marco had given you too much." All eyes were on the man. It was the first time he had spoken to any of them. "I have brought supper and your medicine for the night. It will help you sleep."

Lola took the small plate handed to her. On it was a chunk of bread, a piece of chicken, and broccoli. At least he was giving her decent food to eat. "Line up." He motioned for the girls to form a line in front of him. He held out his hand and Cece took a pill from him. She placed it in her mouth and swallowed. He motioned for her to lift her tongue as he inspected her mouth. *What was she going to do?* He would make sure she was drugged one way or another. She would rather take the pill and stay cognizant of what was happening around her even if she didn't care. Next up was Alisha. Same thing. Dangani was still curled up on her cot. The man signaled Lola was next. She took an apprehensive step forward. She watched as impatience grew on his face. His lips tightened into a thin line, and he raised his brows as if challenging her to disobey him. She trembled but stepped forward.

"What is this?" she asked.

"No questions. Your stay can be pleasant, or it can be hell; it's up to you. You want hell, question me and refuse what I have to give you," the man said, thrusting his hand in front of Lola's chest. Lola wanted pleasant. This was already unpleasant enough as it was. She didn't want to see how much worse it could get. She put the pill on her tongue and swallowed. "Open your mouth and lift your tongue." When the man was satisfied Lola had swallowed the pill, he approached Dangani.

"She has already had enough. Can't you see?" Lola argued with the man. The man stalked towards Lola and backhanded her across her face, knocking her to her cot. She immediately raised a hand to the burning skin.

"Don't question me." He towered over her and raised his hand again to see if she would disobey. Lola slowly sank further into her cot. She watched helplessly as the man pulled a syringe from his pocket and plunged it into Dangani's arm. He then grabbed their bucket and left. Lola sat numbed by the burning and humiliation of being hit. How could they feed them so well but keep them drugged and have a doctor look after them? It didn't make any sense.

A few minutes later, a different man of the same Latino decent entered with their now empty bucket. He placed it in the corner and then he walked within a hair's breadth of Lola. He gestured for her to stand and move to the center of the room. She did. He walked around her, touching her body. She cringed inwardly at the touch but wouldn't show him her fear. She raised her chin defiantly and allowed him to touch her. He lifted her dress and admired her taut stomach. He squeezed her arms and then her thighs, grunting his approval at the toned muscle he felt in his hand. He leaned in and sniffed her. He was dirty and smelled like body odor and urine. She crinkled her nose and breathed through her mouth while he inhaled her. "Honeysuckle," was the only word he spoke. He turned about and left the shack.

CHAPTER FOUR

Rob hit the snooze button on his alarm clock for the fourth and last time. Another morning and he felt like shit. Leaning up slightly, he looked at the time—0730. Staring up at the ceiling, he sighed. *Great, he was going to be late.* Dragging his ass out of bed, he went downstairs and made his way into his kitchen. He poured himself two fingers of scotch and gulped it down. Hair of the dog was the quickest way to put him back into tip-top shape. He needed to be at work by 0900. Running his hands through his hair, he headed to the bathroom and rushed through his shower. At least he hadn't given up on hygiene, except on the weekends. He went to the boxing ring at his local gym regularly to take out his frustration on whatever lucky man happened to want to go a round with him. That kept him in fighting shape. His employment with Blackrain Security required him to stay in the best shape possible. His best asset to the company was that he didn't care if he lived or died. He would gladly step into harm's way to accomplish the mission. And, if he was lucky, it would be the mission which finally reunited him with his Lizzie.

Just the thought of her name had his head spinning. He stood in the shower and remembered the last night they had spent at home. They were watching some chick flick he couldn't remember the name of, but he watched it because it pleased her. She cuddled up to him on the couch and rested her chin against his shoulder. He had his arm draped around her and was caressing her bare skin. She wore her pink boy shorts underwear with a tank top, which left plenty of exposed skin for him to touch. She was remarkably soft and beautiful. He remembered the feel of a tear drop on his bare chest as she cried at the end of the movie. He remembered the way he tilted her chin to thumb away her tears. He remembered the way he slowly made love to her right there on the couch.

He had had his time in paradise; this, his life now, was pure hell.

He got out of the shower more determined than ever to take any and all risks thrown his way today. Heading to his closet, he chose his standard uniform: a pair of jeans that hung perfectly from his narrow hips and showed the briefest hint of the boxer briefs he wore underneath, and a tight fitting t-shirt that showed off his broad shoulders, ripped biceps, and peeked at his half-sleeve tattoo on his right arm snaking onto his chest and right side of his body. Slipping his feet into his work boots, he never bothered to take the time to lace them unless he was on a mission. He didn't give a shit what he looked like, as long as he got the job done. Grabbing his keys from the leaf-like Pier One dish

Lizzie had purchased for that exact reason, he headed out the door.

About forty-five minutes later, Rob reached Blackrain Security. The nondescript brick building housed the company that provided assignments while he and his friends were still self-contractors. Now, all five surviving members of the five tours in Afghanistan were employed by Blackrain, except Kevin who worked for Homeland Security. Blackrain's owner, Rob's boss, was a former Navy SEAL who respected the Green Berets for the grueling training they endured, as well as their success rate while on missions. He waited for Rob at the door.

"You're early. That's shocking," Tyrrell bantered, trying to change the semi-permanent scowl that adorned Rob's face.

"Am I the first one here? That is shocking," Rob said, smiling. It was a start.

"Yeah. I have a job for your team. Let's wait until the others get here, and then I'll brief you all at once. Go get a cup of coffee. You look like you need it," Tyrrell said with an easy smile. Rob walked into the kitchen and was greeted by the company secretary, Helen.

"Good morning, Rob. How did you sleep?" Helen offered Rob black coffee, just the way he liked it.

"Like a baby, Helen," Rob replied. He would never let anyone know he had to pass out from alcohol before he could sleep.

"That's good. We need you in top shape for the new mission. It's a big one," she said with a genuine smile.

Rob walked back down the hallway to the cube farm. He sat at his desk, put his feet up, and drank his coffee while he waited for Tony and Steve to arrive. Michael wouldn't be back to work for two weeks; he was in Aruba on his honeymoon. Rob really was happy for his best friend. He wished he could be a better friend and show it. It's just he was still so raw; it still felt like Lizzie died yesterday. He heard his brothers enter the office and also heard a voice he didn't recognize. He got up and walked to greet his brothers and the new man. He pulled each brother into a one-arm hug and then extended his hand to the stranger. "I'm Rob."

"I'm Aaron. I've been called in for your team," he said and shook Rob's hand.

"I didn't know I was getting anyone new," Rob said, looking to his brothers.

"Neither did we," Tony replied, studying Aaron.

"In my office, please," the boss yelled down the stairs and into the bullpen. Rob led the way. Once in the office, Tyrrell said, "So, I see you met Aaron. I called him in on this mission because we are down a man. Please, everyone have a seat." Tyrrell motioned for the men to sit at the conference table that took up the better portion of his office. Behind the conference table on the back wall were monitors that tracked the comings and goings of the office, as well as Tyrrell's home, inside and out. Downstairs, in the bullpen, were the computers the guys needed. Blackrain Security was a well-respected security firm with ties to the CIA, DOD, NSA, FBI, and DHS. Tyrrell spent a great deal of time shoring up his contact list. He could call on the support of any agency if he needed it.

"So, what is it? Helen said it's big?" Rob questioned.

"How many of you have heard of Americana Airlines?" Tyrrell watched as their faces showed recognition. He caught Rob's eyes. "Well, the CEO and owner of the airline, Peter Sardeson, contacted my office last night after receiving several phone calls from his daughter's friends. Apparently, his daughter, one Lola Sardeson, was out clubbing with three of her girlfriends in Boston the night before last but disappeared from the club. Her girlfriends claim they last saw her dancing with a tall, good looking man of Latino decent. They were occupied and didn't notice her leave the club. It's highly unlikely she would leave the club willingly without her girlfriends, since they all shared a cab. The girls checked her dorm and around campus; she attends Harvard, but they can't locate her. They've called her cell phone, but it goes straight to voicemail. Because the subject is twenty years old, the police aren't willing to touch it yet, which brings us to our mission: Lola Sardeson. Her father is paying double the normal price of hostage retrieval. That means the pay on this is double for each of you." The men smiled at each other.

"Let's get to work. Find out everything you can about the man she was last seen dancing with. Go to

the club, ask around. See if anyone remembers him."
Tyrrell produced a composite sketch the girls had done
from memory. He passed out a copy to each of them.
"It's the closest thing we have to a lead. Take the jet
and see what you can find out. We need a name, and
hopefully that name can lead to an address."

Rob, Steve, Tony, and Aaron arrived in Boston an
hour later and disembarked the private jet—one of the
better perks of working for such a big security
company. They got into the SUV, which was waiting at
the rental agency, and made their way to the Havana
Club. Walking in through the front door, they
immediately headed toward the back. The club wasn't
open yet, but there was someone behind the bar,
stocking up. "Have you seen this man?" Rob asked,
holding the picture under the light shining down from
above the bar.

The bartender looked closer. "Yeah, that's
Miguel. He comes in here every Friday and Saturday
night. Real looker, always leaving with a lady," he
confirmed.

"Would you happen to know Miguel's last
name?" Tony asked.

"No, sorry. I'm not that friendly with any of the
customers. You can wait until Addison arrives. She
works most nights trying to pay her way through
Harvard. She might be able to tell you more."

"Does she work tonight?" Rob asked.

"Yes. Like I said, she rarely takes any days off. She needs the money."

"What's her schedule tonight?" Tony asked, causing the bartender to look up at him.

"The club opens at 7:00 tonight. She usually arrives an hour before to get the place set up."

It was 1700 now. "Mind if we wait around until she gets here?" Rob asserted as he looked directly into the bartender's eyes.

"No skin off of my back. Just have a seat. Can I get you fellas something to drink?"

Rob was the first to respond. "Yeah, I'll have a glass of water." The men looked at him, but they weren't really shocked. He would never drink while on a mission. However, an hour of free time meant an hour to hear Lizzie's cries and watch the movie play in his head.

Like clockwork, Addison arrived at 1800. The men got to their feet and made their way over to where Addison was busily putting her things away in her locker. "Mind if we borrow you for a few minutes?" Rob asked with a smile he knew caused ladies to melt.

"Sure. What's up?" she asked as she tied her black money apron around her hips.

"Have you ever seen this man before? We understand you are here most nights and probably know his name." Tony handed her the sketch.

"This looks a lot like Miguel Perez. He's in here most weekends. Tried picking me up a couple of times, but I'm too busy with school, ya know," she said, giving a Rob a dazzling white smile.

"Thank you, Addison. You've been a great help," Tony said, drawing her attention from Rob.

Once inside the SUV, Rob called the office and gave the name to Tyrrell. Tyrrell ran it through his contacts with various organizations. Several hits came back, but Tyrrell matched the sketch to a specific driver's license. Miguel had a record and a probation officer. That meant his address would be current.

The girls were right. Lola didn't care what was happening. She felt light and unaffected by her situation. Whatever drug they gave her could become addicting, but at the present moment, she didn't care. At first she tried to fight the effects, but it proved to be too powerful.

A man in a white lab coat entered the room. He approached Dangani and examined her vital signs. When he finished looking into her eyes for pupil dilation, he padded his way over to Lola who was sitting on her bed propped up against the bamboo wall. The sun was out again, which meant this was her second day. Today, she would be examined by the doctor. He gathered his stethoscope from around his neck and placed the ear tips in his ears. He placed the chest piece against her chest and listened. He did the same to her back. He shined a very bright light into her eyes that made them water.

"I need you to undress now," the doctor told Lola very matter-of-factly.

Because she was in a current state of mental fog, she didn't care she was undressing in front of a strange man or the other girls. She didn't even care what the man planned on doing to her. She did as instructed and reached for the hem of her dress. She pulled it up over her head. She unclasped the front clasp of her bra and let it fall down her arms to the floor. Next, she hooked her thumbs in the sides of her panties and pulled them down to her feet. The doctor motioned for her to lay her naked body on the filthy mattress. She didn't care; she lay down.

"Spread your legs," the doctor ordered. She watched as he squeezed liquid onto the tips of his two fingers and then felt those fingers press inside her. He didn't press far, and it didn't hurt, not that she would care if it did. She watched as a slow, maniacal grin spread across his face. Something had pleased him. That made her happy. She was glad she had pleased him. She felt even lighter at the thought. Whatever they were drugging her with was working. She could stay in that state forever.

"You can get dressed now," the doctor said as he slapped her bum. She stood and obeyed him. Once she was dressed, she returned to the same position as before he came.

"Are you marking the days?" Alisha asked once the doctor left.

"Yes." Lola pointed to the marks she made with a stone she had found on the floor of the hut. The next pill should be coming soon. "What time do they bring food and medicine?" Lola asked.

"There's no way to tell," Alisha responded. "But don't worry, they don't leave us without medicine for long. They like us this way. We don't fight."

"What do you think they plan to do to us?" Lola asked to make conversation.

"I overheard the men talking a few nights ago, before you arrived. They plan on selling us."

"Selling us to whom?" Lola inquired. She couldn't for the life of her figure out what she would be sold to do.

"Where did you come from?" Alisha asked, confused Lola did not know the implications of that statement. "Why do you think the doctor examines us? To see if we're virgins!" Alisha barked at Lola's ignorance.

Lola still didn't get it. Maybe it was the drugs. Maybe it was her privileged upbringing. Maybe it was her father protecting her from all of the evil in the world. She looked at Alisha, dumbstruck. "They're going to sell us as sex slaves. Virgins fetch a premium," Alisha attested, shocked at Lola's naivety. Everyone knew why virgins commanded a high price.

"What? Sex slaves! When do they plan on selling us?" Lola asked, bewildered.

"The men said the next auction was at the end of the month. I've been here for twenty days. I was taken on the second of July, so less than ten days," Alisha informed her.

"Cece, are you a virgin?" Lola asked.

"Nope, I had a boyfriend before I was taken."

"What about you, Alisha, are you one?"

"Nope, I have had the same boyfriend for two years. We waited until I was sixteen though, so I just lost it this year."

"Does anyone know about Dangani?" Lola looked at the girl still curled into a fetal position on the cot. Lola got up and went to her, sitting down next to her. She stroked her forehead and said, "Dangani?" Dangani looked up at Lola with bright, wide eyes. Her pupils were unnaturally large. "Dangani, are you still a virgin?"

"The men raped me before they brought me here." Dangani's eyes glistened with unshed tears. No wonder she was so quiet. She went through a brutal experience at the tender age of thirteen.

"Why would they rape her if virgins fetch a higher fee?" Lola asked, still stroking Dangani's forehead, comforting her.

"It all depends on where you live and who takes you. Some people are all about the money, some not," Cece responded. "Where were you taken from?" She looked at Lola.

"A Boston nightclub, in front of a large group of people. They threatened my friends with death if I didn't go," Lola recalled almost absentmindedly. "What about you guys? Where were you taken from?" Lola asked her fellow captives.

"I was taken from a mall in Florida," Alisha responded.

"And I was taken from a museum in France," Cece said.

Lola turned her attention back to Dangani. "Where were you taken from?"

"A market with my mother not ten feet away from me." Dangani began to cry.

40

Lola's medicine must have worn off because, for the first time since she arrived, she felt fear. She was afraid of being sold. Afraid of the man who would purchase her. Afraid she would never live out her dream of having a family. Afraid for the other girls in the room. Lola and Dangani wept in silence.

STRONGER

Rob stared at the ceiling. He didn't drink last night, which meant he didn't sleep either. He rolled over and looked at the clock—0500 hours. That suited him just fine. His roommate, Tony, was still asleep on the other double bed. Rob got up and made his way into the hotel bathroom. He turned the water to scalding and stepped under the spray. He stood there for a while thinking of his Lizzie. He recalled the way her short hair stuck up so adorably in the mornings when she would wake up. He remembered how she always had coffee waiting for him downstairs; she was an early riser. Pushing the thoughts to the back of his mind, he lathered up. When he was done washing and rinsing his hair, he stepped out and quickly dried himself off. He wrapped the towel around his hips and headed back into the room to get dressed. Tony was sitting up when he entered the room.

"Good morning," Tony mumbled, still half asleep. If they were going to surprise Miguel Lopez, it would be early in the morning while he was still asleep. They spent the rest of last night gathering the supplies they would need to interrogate Lopez if he refused to talk. As Tony made his way into the bathroom to grab a shower, Rob dropped the towel and quickly dressed in his standard gear. This time he laced his boots and would be wearing a bullet-proof vest—company policy. He waited until Tony was dressed before he called Steve and Aaron's room. They were ready and waiting.

"Meet downstairs in ten. We'll grab a quick breakfast and hit Lopez around 0630 hours," Rob told them. Ten minutes later they met in the lobby. The men loaded up on hard boiled eggs and cereal. They talked strategy, and fifteen minutes later, they were ready to go.

Rob typed in Lopez's current address. The GPS said twenty-eight minutes. They followed the directions and parked two houses down from Lopez's. Thank God it was still early or they would have an audience. The men gathered at the back of the van and each placed a Sig 226 behind their backs, using their shirts to hide the weapons. They cautiously approached the house.

"Steve and Aaron, you go around front. Tony you're on my six." Rob pulled out his lock-picking tools and picked the back sliding glass door lock. Rob could pick any lock, one of the many skills he picked up as a Green Beret. He slowly slid the glass door ajar and waited. He made a fist and held it above his head, indicating for Tony to be still and silent. They stood for a full thirty seconds listening for sounds. All was quiet. He stepped into the living room and the floor board creaked. He made the same hand sign to Tony and waited again. When he still didn't hear anything, he entered the ranch home.

Rob led the way down the hallway to the bedroom doors. He carefully turned the knob of the first door and peeked inside: empty. He headed towards the second door, repeating the procedure, and found his target. He walked quietly into the room and Tony followed. Together they caged Lopez in with Tony standing in front of the door and Rob getting ready to make contact. With lightning speed, Rob rolled Lopez over, climbed onto the bed, and pressed a knee to Lopez's back.

"What the fuck?" Lopez cried.

"Shut the fuck up!" Rob shouted as he struggled to bring Lopez's right arm up and pin it with his free hand. He did the same with his other arm. In minutes, Rob had Lopez's hands zip-tied behind his back with minimum effort.

"What the fuck do you want? I haven't done anything," Lopez professed as Rob forced him into a sitting position.

"We need to ask you a few questions," Rob replied, a serious scowl on his face.

"And what? You couldn't knock?" Lopez all but spat at Rob. Tony had his gun pulled and trained on Lopez.

"Do yourself a favor and answer our questions, and we won't need to get serious with you," Rob said with a look of menace in his eyes.

"I'll answer anything! I have nothing to hide," Lopez assured the man pointing the gun at him. Rob pulled Lopez to his feet.

"Let's go to the kitchen. I need to get the front door," Rob explained, leading Lopez into the kitchen with Tony bringing up the rear. Rob opened the front door and motioned for Steve and Aaron to enter.

"Let's get the supplies," Rob said. "Tony, stay here with him," he ordered as he headed back out the door with Steve and Aaron. The men made their way to the van where they pulled a piece of plywood, a bucket, and a thick towel out from the back. They carried it into Lopez's living room and leaned the plywood against the wall.

"Why do you need that?" Lopez raised his chin, pointing to the plywood.

"That's in case you don't want to talk." Tony smiled.

"Ask me anything," Lopez shot back. He was starting to look more defiant by the minute.

"Where did you take Ms. Sardeson?" Rob asked quietly.

"Who?" Lopez replied, looking confused.

"You were the last one seen with her on Saturday evening at The Havana Club. So, I will ask you again. Where did you take her?" Rob inquired a little more seriously this time.

Lopez met Rob's stare. "I have no idea what you're talking about."

"We already placed you with her on Saturday night. Three of her friends saw you, as well as a waitress at the club. So, if you don't want to use that board over there," Rob said, pointing to the board, "I suggest you tell us where you took her."

Just then Rob's phone started vibrating in his pocket. He looked at Tony, silently asking him to stand guard while he hit the green button on his smartphone. "Yeah, kind of busy here," he said in way of a greeting.

"I have important information you need before you start interrogating Lopez," Tyrrell replied. "Remember how I said our boy has a record? Well, my contact just sent his FBI record over to me. Apparently, Lopez is on their radar. You will be interested in the fact that your boy there is a scout for a major Mexican drug cartel: the Ortiz Cartel. According to my source, not only do they sell drugs, but they are also rumored to sell underage girls to buyers around the world."

"Fuck," Rob mumbled into the phone. "Why haven't they picked him up yet?"

"He hasn't shown his hand. He is very good at delivering merchandise. They haven't been able to catch him. They also want to see what he can lead them to. Bigger fish so to speak," Tyrrell countered.

"Do you think this is what we are dealing with? A goddamn trafficking ring?" Rob asked, pacing a hole in the already worn, cheap carpet stained with God only knew what.

"Her father sent me a picture right after you guys were asleep for the night. She is a knockout with a killer body. And the way her father talks about her, I wouldn't be surprised if she was out sowing some wild oats Saturday night. Apparently, Daddy kept his little girl sheltered her entire life. That was until Lola started Harvard. Then, he admitted, it was harder to control her whereabouts and associations," Tyrrell informed him.

"So, our simple mission just turned into an international, complicated one. Fuck, the longer we don't get answers, the longer she is missing, the more harm could come to her," Rob stated matter-of-factly. "And what about the FBI? Are we turning this over to them?"

"No. They don't want it yet. They don't want to get involved with the Mexican government unless they have concrete proof, and so far, they don't. To them, this is just a girl that ran away from the stressors of life. They are willing to provide support once we can provide them with proof," Tyrrell assured Rob. Rob's instincts, which were never wrong, said Lopez knew exactly where Lola Sardeson was.

"Thanks, Tyrrell. I'll be in touch." Rob disconnected the call. "Gentlemen," Rob said, motioning the men into the living room. Rob informed them of his telephone conversation and then stalked back to Lopez. "This is your last chance to do this the easy way. Where did you take the girl from Saturday night?"

"I didn't take anybody anywhere. I was at the club dancing, having a few drinks, flirting a little. What's the big deal?" Lopez chided.

"The big deal is the girl you were last seen with and whom, might I mention again, was last seen with you, has disappeared." Rob looked at Tony. "Bring the board."

Tony brought the board into the kitchen and dragged the table to the counter. He placed the plywood on top of the counter and slanted it down to rest on the table. "Bring him here." Rob motioned for Aaron to escort Lopez to the board. Rob and Aaron lifted Lopez onto the board so his head was pointing down the slope.

"Get the towel." Steve handed Rob the towel and stood ready with a full bucket of water. Rob placed the towel over Lopez's face, taking care to cover his nose and his mouth. Then Rob began pouring water into the towel. Rob continued to pour until he could hear gurgling. He stopped and placed the bucket on the ground before he removed the wet towel from Lopez. "Where did you take her?" Rob demanded.

"Go fuck yourself," Lopez spat.

"Again," Rob said as Tony poured the contents of the full bucket on the towel. Rob, for all intents and purposes, practically drowned Lopez three times before Lopez caved.

The men helped Lopez back to the chair. "Talk," Rob barked.

"I asked her to leave the club with me. I brought her back here. We had sex, and then she left. I haven't seen her since."

"Again," Rob demanded as the men lifted Lopez back onto the board. They tortured him twice more before Rob felt he finally had had enough and would tell the truth. But in all actuality, they could keep this up all day. Rob had to give Lopez credit. He didn't think it would take five times to get to the truth. And Rob's instincts said this guy knew the truth, or he would never have tortured him in the first place.

Back at the kitchen chair, out of breath, water dripping from his face, an exhausted Lopez struggled to breathe. "I took her. I delivered her to a private airstrip outside of Boston where she boarded a plane headed for Mexico," he finally confessed.

"How much money did you receive for delivering her?" Rob asked, hoping Lopez's struggle to breathe would afford him to be much more upfront with him.

"I haven't been paid yet. I won't be until the auction."

Rob turned ghost white upon realization of what Lopez had revealed.

"Fuck. I want the address of that airfield, and I want to know what time you dropped her off and to whom." Rob looked straight into Lopez's frightened eyes. Lopez's eyes widened.

"If I tell you that, I am as good as dead," he pleaded.

"You're dead if you don't," Rob calculated.

A pregnant moment of silence passed as Rob stared Lopez down. At that particular moment, he would have no problem killing a man who kidnapped girls and sold them into the sex-slave trade.

"I dropped her off to Luis around 2:00 am. She got on the plane, and that's the last I've seen of her."

"What airfield?" Rob forced through clenched teeth. He would love nothing more than to put a bullet through this bastard's forehead.

"Lowell airfield. The military base closed a long time ago. That's the strip they use." Lopez sunk his head, accepting his defeat.

Other than the fact that the carpet was now a puddle, the men cleaned up their supplies and made it look like they were never there. They loaded the van and left a present for the FBI.

Rob dialed Tyrrell. "Lowell Airport. That's where he dropped her. We need flight information to find the traveler, Luis. We are en route to Lowell now. Yeah, we left him tied up and waiting for the FBI. Okay, I will wait for your call." Rob disconnected with Tyrrell.

STRONGER

CHAPTER
SEVEN

Lola left Dangani's side and made it to her cot before the man entered. She didn't want to be seen giving her attention; she was leery of how her captors would feel about that.

"Stand up. I measure you," the man demanded of the girls in the hut. One by one the girls stood. Lola stepped forward. "Lift arms." Lola did as she was told and lifted her trim arms above her head. The man measured around her breasts, fondling and touching as he did so. Next, he measured her inseam, purposely brushing between her legs. God, these were good drugs. She didn't care she was being touched where no man had touched her before. "I bring back clothes. You try on and model for Mr. Ortiz," the man said as he noted her measurements in his black notebook.

As promised, the man returned, but not before food and medicine. Lola's belly was nice and full, and her medicine calmed her and made her feel like she was floating around the room. The man entered with an armful of negligees. He gave each girl six different nighties to try and model. Thank God she didn't care, but in the back of her mind she told herself she wouldn't be caught dead doing this in front of a man, let alone a stranger. One by one the girls were escorted outside the hut to the main house. She giggled when she saw the pretentious lion statues which guarded the gold-plated entrance door. This place was a fort. Everywhere she looked, men with machine guns stood guard. She passed four of them on the way to the main house and saw another two standing behind the lion statues.

She entered the house and was immediately taken back to her father's world: all marble floors and gold chandeliers. The opulence was disgusting, but then again, she didn't care. She was led up the curved staircase to a long hallway. Each girl was placed in a room. She had no idea what she would have to do. She just hoped the drugs didn't wear off while she was doing it. The man who placed her in the room told her to put on an outfit and then disappeared. She heard the lock click behind him. She chose a red satin camisole, which barely covered her ass, and quickly got dressed. It dipped low in the front, revealing her generous, perky breasts. She could see her nipples through the fabric.

The room was decorated in pale golds and dark greens; she thought it looked gaudy. She walked to the large, stately window and moved back the thick gold drapery to peer outside. She watched absentmindedly as the guards paced back and forth across the grounds. She noticed several huts along the back wall of forest. She could tell the grounds were surrounded, at least on her side, by thick forest. As she was standing looking out of the window, she heard the door open. She turned around suddenly and was startled by a small Latino looking man with a gringo mustache. Although the top of his head was bald, the sides of his hair were longer, and he sported a bad comb-over. She giggled seeing the gel holding his hair in place reflecting the room's artificial light. He had a pot belly, the kind one gets from drinking too much, and wore suspenders to hold his chinos in place. She giggled again. A thought that perhaps she should be afraid of this man popped into her head, but it was gone just as quickly.

The man approached her, but she was rooted to the spot in which she stood. Fear—the thought was back. He removed the unlit, half-chewed cigar from his mouth and made a grunting noise, which came from the back of his throat. He did not speak, which increased her anxiety level. *What did he plan on doing?* It had only been three or four hours since her last pill, but she was starting to feel fear. It was because she was being devoured by his eyes. He started at her feet and slowly perused his way to the top of her head. He approached closer now, and she cringed back into herself. He picked up a strand of her long, golden blond hair and twisted it around his chubby finger. He pulled her head down by his finger and deeply inhaled. He held up the white negligee and handed it to her. She took it and clenched it against her chest. She really didn't want this creepy man looking at her naked.

The man waited patiently, chewing on his cigar. When she didn't move, he walked over and grabbed the white negligee out of her hands and threw it on the bed. A shudder moved through her as he ran his hand down between her breasts and over her pubic area until he reached the hem of the red satin. With both hands, he pulled it over her head. She trembled and stared at the ground. She couldn't look into his eyes; he scared her. He picked up the discarded white negligee and handed it to her, again patiently waiting for her to do the honors. She quickly pulled it over her body, not that it did any good. Only the trim was outlined in silk, every other part of the white mesh negligee was see-through. He stared at her, ogling her breasts. *Why did it have to be so cold in this room?* He motioned for her to turn around and she obeyed. This time he motioned and said the word, "Slowly." Again, she did as he demanded.

He walked up to her until she could smell the liquor and chewed tobacco on his breath. She would never again be able to smell that scent and not think of this man. He kept walking forward, into her, causing her to bump the back of her legs against the bed. With one small, swollen hand, he pushed her onto the bed until she was spread beneath him. *This was not good.* She needed the drugs to endure this. He spread her legs and placed both hands solidly on her knees indicating for her not to move. She wasn't wearing panties. *What was he doing?*

He opened the bedside table and pulled out a bottle of gel lubricant, the kind she had seen the doctor use. He returned to her and placed two lubed fingers inside her center. She squeezed her legs together to try to stop him, but he wedged his short body in-between her knees to keep them open. When he felt her hymen still intact, he smirked. He removed his fingers and began to circle her clit. She thrashed her head from side to side trying to ignore the fact that he was touching a place no man had ever touched before. She always thought she would get to choose the man who touched her there.

Her pulse started to race. She clenched her jaw and tried to ignore what he was doing to her. It didn't feel good; it felt wrong. She felt a pain deep in her chest, but she ignored it. She tried very hard to hide her terror from him, but it was no use. He saw her fear. He saw her shrink into herself as if trying to hide. She squeezed her legs together again, trying to limit his access. This time she pressed firmly against the man's legs. He continued to lazily circle her clit, but when he could tell he wasn't turning her on, he stopped. She exhaled. He extended his hand, the one that had been inside her, to her and waited until she placed her hand in his. Then he pulled her up to a sitting position. He lifted her arms and removed the white negligee from her now naked body. She had never felt such humiliation. Such degradation. Such violation.

"Raphael," the man yelled. A second later, the man who had originally brought her the clothes was back in the room with her. The man handed Raphael the white negligee and then exited the room.

"Get dressed now," Raphael said before exiting the room. She wondered if the other girls were going through this same type of disgrace. She dressed and went back to the window. She wrapped her arms around the middle of her body and stayed, gazing out at the grounds, until she was led back to the hut.

CHAPTER
EIGHT

Rob and the rest of the team made their way to
Lowell Airfield. They parked their SUV at a clearing
in the woods surrounding the airfield. They had to
sneak in to capture Luis, the delivery man for the Ortiz
Cartel. The men exited the vehicle with purpose.
Rounding the back of the SUV, they reached in and
grabbed AR-15 assault weapons. They loaded extra
ammo into the field pockets on their vests and pants.
Once they were ready, they made the half-mile hike to
the entrance of the airfield.

"I hope this asshole is waiting for another run. I
don't want to be stuck here on surveillance until he
returns," Rob commented to the men as they reached
the entrance. A barbed-wire fence protected the airfield
from intrusion. *How were Ortiz's men getting in here?*
There had to be an opening. Walking the fence, about a
quarter of a mile into the woods, Steve found a hole
big enough for one man to crawl through. Luckily, the
Ortiz men hadn't wanted to be spotted either, so the
entrance was blocked by an old, boarded-up brick
building. They entered the field behind a tan brick
building with paint flaking from the exposed brick.

In tight formation, the men hugged the back wall and then, when they were sure it was clear, the side of the building. Looking around, Rob could see four airplane hangars about a mile in the distance. They would have to cross two runways completely in the open. There were no buildings to hide them. They had to pray if Ortiz's men were here, they were stashed in a closed hangar.

Rob looked at the men. "Are you ready? We have about a mile of open space to cross."

"What if we walk the perimeter and enter the hangars from the back," Tony asked. Rob always liked his ideas.

"It will take three times as long, but it won't give away our position. What do you think, Steve?" Rob asked.

"I'm all for keeping our position secure. I don't care if it takes all night to reach the hangars," Steve uttered excitedly.

"That settles it. Tony, you take point. We'll bring up your six. Let's try not to fire our weapons, if at all possible. I want to take Luis and his men by surprise." Rob stepped to the side so Tony could take lead. The men began jogging, hugging the fence, under the cover of the old buildings and overgrown vegetation.

Rob noticed the magnificent pinks, purples, and oranges that blazed in the sky as the sun began to set. He looked at his watch—2045 hours; it was a perfect summer evening. He recalled with clarity the last summer evening he had spent with Lizzie. How they sipped red wine on their deck. Nothing special, just a night like any other. They had just finished a wonderful dinner. Rob had manned the grill and Lizzie took care of the salad and sides. After they finished their meal, they sat in silence watching the sun dip below the horizon. He remembered the look in her eyes as she said, "Isn't it beautiful? This is my favorite time of night." Rob glanced at her expression as she looked off into the distance. This was his favorite part of the night, too. Just the two of them, after their chores were complete, simply enjoying each other's company. He placed his hand on her knee and trailed his fingers up her thigh. She met his gaze when his fingertips made it to her center. She smiled sweetly at him and took the same path up his leg until her hand was covering his erection. She gave a mischievous smile and stood. He followed her into the house and upstairs to the bedroom. She slowly undressed for him, piece by piece. They made love all night and fell asleep in each other's arms.

"Let's clear the first one," Aaron said, bringing Rob out of his reverie. He couldn't afford to be drifting off on a mission. He shook his head and crouched at the opening of the back door as Aaron picked the lock. Aaron went through the open door and Rob brought up his gun. The building was pitch black. No one occupied it. "Shall we have a closer look, just to be safe?" Aaron brought up his gun as Rob stepped past him into the large, dark space. The men donned their night vision goggles. They proceeded to make their way from the back of the building to the front, inspecting each office as they went.

"Clear," Rob yelled just loud enough for the other men to hear. He began walking back the way he had come.

When they opened the door to the third building, Rob crouched and pointed his gun. When Aaron breached the door, Rob was pointing his gun directly at the back of a man's head. Rob held up his fist. Rob pulled out his knife from his bootstrap holster and cautiously and quietly approached the man. Rob didn't make a sound. With one move, Rob brought his hand around the neck of the man holstering a weapon and sliced his neck from ear to ear. There was a loud gurgling sound as blood sputtered out of the man's mouth. Rob quietly lowered the man to the concrete floor. They removed their night-vision goggles. Once Rob cleared Ortiz's guard, he motioned for the men to enter noiselessly. There was a large airplane standing between Rob and the voices he heard coming from the other side.

"I hear four distinct voices," Rob whispered to his men.

"So do I," Tony agreed. "Let's assume there are two that aren't talking."

"We need to take Luis alive. Steve and I will hide. Tony and Aaron, you get yourselves caught. That way we'll find out where Luis is before we kill everyone." Rob gestured to each of the men.

"Why do I always have to be the one to get caught?" Tony questioned with a look of devilment in his eyes. It was true; every mission that required this tactic, Rob always volunteered Tony.

"You're so good at it, brother," Rob bantered.

Rob watched from his hiding spot as Tony and Aaron made their way, guns drawn, to the men at the front of the hangar. "Don't shoot," Tony warned the men. "Ortiz sent us as reinforcements. There is going to be trouble tonight," Tony said to Ortiz's men.

"Why didn't I know about this?" a man asked, aiming his gun at Tony's head.

"Don't ask us. Ask Ortiz. We were hired to be extra security for the shipment, which is coming in tonight," Tony said, keeping his gun trained on the man. "Which one of you is Luis? We were told to check in with him."

Rob had taken up position behind one wheel well, giving him a clear view of the front of the room. He was a marksman when it came to his assault weapon. He could clear the room before Tony or Aaron had a chance to be captured.

Luis stepped forward. "I am. Who did you say hired you?"

"We didn't," Tony quipped as he lunged for Luis.

Rob fired his first round, taking down the man to Luis's right. Steve's bullet took out the second man who was standing guard at Luis's left. They made quick work, two rapid bullets, and the other two men were taken down without a bullet wasted. Signaling the all-clear, Steve followed Rob from behind the airplane. Tony and Steve had managed to disarm a shocked Luis and zip-tie his hands behind his back as Rob and Steve appeared.

"You have no idea how much shit you just brought on yourselves," Luis spat in Rob's direction.

"I think it's you that should be worried," Rob said with a cold calm that overtook him in the heat of a battle. "Grab him." Rob pointed to the dead man lying to his left. "You're going to pose for some pictures," Rob told Luis as a slow smile spread across his face. "And if that doesn't work, we will resort to extreme measures," Rob continued.

"Ortiz will hunt you down and kill your families," Luis spat out.

"What family?" Rob grunted as he pulled the pants off of the dead man. "Sit him down." Rob pointed to Luis. Luis was now seated on the cold, concrete floor of the hangar. "Just like we used to do," Rob reminisced with Steve and Tony. Tony squeezed Luis's cheeks together, effectively prying open his mouth. Rob stood at the ready. This was the part he didn't like, but the results were usually the same. Tony had forced Luis onto his back, turning his face to the side. Rob positioned the dead man's crotch in front of Luis's face. Rob picked up the man's penis and placed it in Luis's mouth. Luis gagged and coughed, trying desperately to turn his head. "Smile," Steve said, standing over Luis's body as he held the cell phone camera overhead.

As Luis coughed and gagged, Rob removed the penis from Luis's mouth. "Now cooperate and no one will ever see what appears to be you giving this man here a blow job."

"That doesn't frighten me. What frightens me is Ortiz." Luis raised his chin now that Tony had let him go.

"What should frighten you is me and my three bad-ass, motherfucking brothers here who have been trained to get information from reluctant participants. That man's dick in your mouth was for our amusement. We'll show this picture to your family. In fact, my man Tony here will broadcast it all over the Internet, and it will go viral within the hour," Rob said in his most menacing voice. "What do you think, men, more pictures first?"

"We could have him butt-fuck that dead guy." Tony laughed.

Rob was a cold, sadistic bastard, but after everything he had seen and witnessed, after all of his harsh training and the brutality of five tours, after losing his Lizzie, he really didn't give a fuck anymore. Anything went. In fact, he would start with the fingers instead of the fingernails. He easily rationalized Luis was nothing more than the scum on the bottom of his shoe. He sold young, innocent girls into the sex-slave trade. Nope, Rob didn't feel sad, sorry, or even guilty for what he did or was about to do to this piece of shit.

Rob reached down and removed Luis's shoes. Then he pulled Luis pants off his legs. "Flip him over." Rob pointed to the dead man with no pants. Tony flipped him onto his stomach. Aaron and Steve helped Luis to his knees and positioned him so it would look like he was butt fucking the dead man. "Smile pretty. This one goes on the Internet tonight." Rob laughed as he snapped a couple of pictures of the man mimicking the sexual position. "I've had my fun. Let's cut to the chase. Where are the girls from your shipment of a week ago? We know you get your shipments on Saturday nights and fly them out shortly after they arrive."

It pained Rob to talk about innocent, young girls like they were nothing but cargo. They were someone's daughter, someone's sister, someone's love. They didn't deserve to be sold just because they were easily attainable or neglected by family. No girl deserved that. In his book, girls and women should be revered, especially the innocent ones. Sure he slept with his fair share of women and always left before they could awake in the morning, but he was always upfront and always gave his women more pleasure than they could stand.

Rob had better snap out of his thoughts or he was going to kill Luis before he had the information he needed to rescue Lola Sardeson. "Grab a chair," Rob barked. Tony brought the chair from the office and sat it in front of Rob. Tony and Steve transferred Luis to the comfortable, cushiony office chair. "You comfortable?" Rob coldly asked Luis with a look of death and fury in his eyes.

"Get me the branch cutters from the bag, please," Rob asked Steve. Steve returned from the back of the hangar with a black bag that had all kinds of fun little tools they could use on Luis. "I am going to start with your fingers. I don't have time to shit around." Rob held the orange tree branch cutters in his right hand by the black handle. He closed the distance to Luis in three long strides. "Hold his hand flat over the armrest."

With Luis's fingers protruding over the end of the arm rest, Rob started with his forefinger. He placed the sharp metal blades and brought the handles of the cutters together slightly, just enough to cut the skin. "Tell me where the girls go once they leave here, and I will stop," Rob implored Luis. But Luis remained tight lipped. He had drawn his lips into thin lines and his jaw worked back and forth as if he was grinding his teeth against the pain. Fresh tears sprung to his eyes. Rob brought the handles of the cutters together, cutting at the joint of Luis's forefinger. Luis screamed and squeezed his eyes shut. Blood was quickly pooling on the concrete floor.

"We can't have you bleeding to death before we get our answers, now can we, Luis?" Rob said as he retrieved a blow torch from the black bag. He turned it on high. Reaching into the bag, he pulled out a flat piece of metal no bigger than a book. He took the torch and heated the end of the metal until it glowed red. Grabbing the cooler end of the metal with pliers, he placed the glowing end against Luis's nub of meat. The smell of burnt flesh quickly filled Rob's nostrils, and Luis's screams quickly filled his ears. "Had enough yet?" Rob asked.

Luis's eyes were raining tears. Rob barely had enough time to jump out of the way as Luis lurched forward and vomited into the pool of blood on the dusty floor. "I always forget about that part," Rob said, smiling. Once Luis was done, Rob asked the same question. "Tell me where the girls go from here." Apparently, Luis was a weak man, because it only took the removal and cauterizing of one finger and Luis was spilling his guts.

"They go to the personal property of Ortiz. He has huts he keeps them in until they are sold," Luis said through thick and heavy breaths.

"How long does he keep them before he sells them?" Rob asked.

Luis brought his breath back under control and tightened his lips again. At the sight of Luis being closed lipped, Rob reached for the cutters. "You know, I really have no problem with this. If I run out of fingers, I just move to the toes. Then there are other body parts I save for the truly tough ones." Luis remained tight lipped. Rob brought the cutters and positioned them over Luis's middle finger. He applied pressure as he squeezed the handles tighter. Luis's middle finger flung across the room. It really was amazing what one could do with the right tools. He brought the blow torch up to heat the metal and cauterize Luis's stub.

"Stop!" Luis shouted. "I will tell you anything you want to know. No more. I can't take any more," Luis begged of Rob.

Rob looked at Steve, Tony, and Aaron with pride glinting in his gray eyes. Rob was known as one of the most effective interrogators the Army had ever seen. He could break even the toughest man in a matter of hours. Rob had a knack for knowing what to start with and what would cause the least amount of damage but yield the highest results. It truly was his gift.

"How long does Ortiz keep the girls?" Rob demanded.

"About twenty days. First they see a doctor and then a shopper. That way they look their best on auction day. He doesn't drug them up on auction day either. He is sadistic like that." Luis was telling all. He was answering questions Rob wasn't even going to ask.

"Where are the auctions held?" Rob asked, realizing Lola Sardeson was probably getting ready to head to auction now.

"Colonia Hidalgo. About thirty minutes from his property," Luis replied. "Do you want the address?"

Stunned, Rob nodded his head. He really did have a way with torture.

"There's a farm at the northeast end of town. They hold the auction in a barn. Well, it only looks like a barn. Inside is something else. Each man is assured anonymity by the two-way mirror in a private room which separates him from the auction floor. The girls are paraded outside each mirror, one at a time, and the bidding begins. Usually, there is a packed house on auction night. Ortiz's girls are mostly virgins, so they fetch a premium bid, always six figures." Rob was shaking his head in disbelief at Luis's words. He couldn't think about what the men did once they purchased the girls, or he would be sick.

Rob reached into his pocket and pulled out his phone. He dialed Tyrrell and quickly communicated the information to him. They would need to regroup and strategize.

Once the FBI arrived, Rob turned over Luis to an agent. The agent eyed Rob suspiciously when he looked at the blackened nubs of Luis's hand. Rob ignored the look and proceeded to the SUV with the men. Time was of the essence.

"Dangani? How are you feeling?" Lola asked as the dark box truck she and the other girls rode in bounced up and down over the rough roads.

"I'm scared. What is going to happen to us?" Dangani grasped Lola's hand and squeezed. In a reassuring gesture, Lola squeezed back.

"I overheard the guards saying they were moving us to the farm today. They didn't give me any pills. Did any of you get yours?" Lola asked, confident the answer was no.

"No, just a small piece of bread and some water," Cece replied from the other side of the box truck. "Did you hear what waits for us at the farm?"

The floor of the truck was gritty to the touch. Upon entering, they were ordered to sit up against the walls. The truck bobbed and weaved, and so did Lola's body. She was swaying back and forth and landed on her rear each time the truck hit a ditch. She was sore from the ride. She steadied herself by placing her right hand against the floor as the truck came to a stop. This stop was longer than a stop-sign stop. She reckoned they were at the farm. It had been a short trip. If she had to guess, she would say thirty minutes. Dangani began whimpering, and Lola placed her arm around her small shoulders, pulling her close and hugging her. The back door opened, and sunlight flooded the box. Lola could see the fear in each of the girls' eyes. This was the end of the line. Their destiny awaited them inside the barn. Lola helped Dangani to stand.

"Don't let them see you cry," Lola whispered to Dangani. Lola watched as Dangani's features transformed into defiance. She raised her chin and wiped her cheeks with the back of her hand. One by one they were led on into the pasture. There was a rundown farmhouse to the right of where the truck had stopped. Shutters hung sideways from the windows. Paint peeled off the house like skin peeling off a sunburned shoulder. Lola could see the screen door was badly in need of repair as the top half ripped away from the door and folded over the bottom half.

The girls—Lola counted twelve in all—stood in the middle of the pasture. *Were they brought here to work on the man's farm?* That wouldn't make sense. *Why did they bring them here?* When the truck moved and a guard appeared with an assault rifle in his hand and tucked under his arm, Lola swallowed down the panic that quickly rose in her throat. She had no idea what awaited them, but at least they were still together. She could watch over Dangani, Cece, and Alisha. The armed guard gestured with the barrel of his gun for the girls to move towards the big red barn in the distance.

It was strange that the barn was in immaculate condition; at least the outside looked that way. A fresh coat of bright, fire-engine red paint coated it. The doors were kept closed by a metal bar which hooked into a latch on each door. Lola easily recognized the smell of cow manure she remembered from her country drives with her family. She even picked up a faint trace of hay. Why did they want the girls in the barn? *Would they be taken somewhere else?*

The other guard opened the metal lever and swung the right door open. The sun was still high overhead, so Lola judged it to be around one o'clock in the afternoon. The heat was unbearable. Sweat already trickled down her brow and between her bosom. She felt droplets dribble down her back. She was still dressed in the short, blue mini-dress she had worn to the club over a week ago. Now the dress was grungy with the same dust covering the fabric from the hut. It was a clingy dress that showed off all of her curves.

When she left her hut this morning, the marks under her bed showed she'd been held captive for ten days. They had fed her well and kept her medicated. She didn't want to admit to herself that she needed the drugs to cope. She dreaded turning into her mother, but the circumstances were vastly different. She was being held hostage. She did need the drugs to cope because not knowing what was coming was scaring her to death. She recalled a conversation she heard a few days earlier from the guards in front of her cabin. At the time, she didn't care. But now, she had to remember exactly what they were saying because her instincts said that was the answer to what was going to happen to them.

She racked her brain trying to recall the words spoken in Spanish. Thank God her father insisted she take it starting in elementary school. She could speak it fluently and could understand it just as well. What had they said? Suddenly, dread crept up her spine like fingernails on a chalk board. She was hyperaware of what was going on around her. She noticed the man who had opened the barn door was now standing behind them. She tried to peek into the barn, but it was dark, and the blinding sunlight prevented her from seeing inside. She was aware of where all of the men were. They all had guns slung over their shoulders, and some men had guns hanging from their sides. *Would they kill her if she tried to run?* She was readying for the run when Cece pulled her back.

"What's wrong, Lola?" Cece asked, quickly grabbing Lola's hand. "Your face went so pale. You look like you saw a ghost." Cece stroked Lola's long hair down her back, trying to calm her.

"I am going to be…" That was all Lola could say before she fell to her knees, wrapped her arms around her stomach, and vomited up the bread and water she'd had for breakfast. Cece remained dutifully by her side, holding her hair back from her face. Once the heaves stopped, Lola turned her head and looked up at Cece. Lola's blue eyes were as dark as a storm cloud. She remembered what the men had said. "Oh no," Lola groaned, keeping eye contact with Cece. Lola looked at all of the young girls that stood around her waiting to enter the barn. Tears instantly formed in her eyes. She began sobbing.

"You're scaring me," Cece whimpered.

Lola cried for what was going to be done to her. Lola cried for the loss of innocence the younger girls would face. But most of all, Lola cried for her new friend Dangani who was only thirteen years old. Some man was going to own her as his personal sex slave. Still on her knees, Lola began chanting a prayer over and over to God. "Please. Please. Please."

Lola was the last to reluctantly enter the barn. What struck her first was the catwalk closed in on both sides by dark paneled glass. She couldn't see what was behind the glass. Lola followed the girls onto the catwalk and behind the professional looking stage from which the catwalk extended. The girls were led back into a large room with mirrors and dressing tables on each side of the room. It looked like a large dressing room the stars had used when she had been invited backstage during a Broadway performance of *The Lion King*. Laid out on each dressing table were cosmetics, brushes, combs, hair products, hair bows, barrettes—anything one would need to make oneself attractive. In the middle of the room was a large mobile rack filled with negligees hanging from padded hangers. This is what the man who measured her had been doing: securing clothing for each girl to wear at the auction. Just then she noticed that same man with a small army of Latino women enter the dressing room.

"First you shower. Then we will get you ready for tonight. Tonight is the big night, ladies," the man cooed. The girls looked at each other with panic-filled eyes.

"The big night for what?" Cece whispered to Lola. Lola didn't want to tell Cece, but she would want to know.

"They are selling us tonight," Lola said, defeated, as her shoulders slumped forward. She had surrendered to what was to come. She reached out to grab Cece's arm, refusing to let go.

"Selling us for what?" Cece asked, confused. "You're hurting me."

"Sorry. I just don't know how you are going to handle what I am about to tell you." Lola still had her fingers wrapped around Cece's arm, just not as tight. "Men are going to buy us and then we will belong to them. They will do with us as they please." Lola waited and watched as her words began to register on Cece's face. Cece paled.

"I'm going to be sick. I need a bathroom. I don't think I can hold it in," Cece said, panicked. Her breathing had increased and was coming out in short spurts.

"We need a bathroom. She's going to be sick," Lola announced to the measurement man. He pointed. Lola grabbed Cece by the hand and pulled her back through the door the man pointed to. Lola held Cece's hair this time and stroked her back. So young. The thought of the virgins among the group had taken Lola aback. She thought of herself, still a virgin, naively waiting for the right man. To lose something so special to a man who was obviously a sick degenerate, to a man who wouldn't be gentle, to a man who didn't care for any of the girls, made Lola's face burn with anger.

Lola began to shake with her rage, but what could she do? What she would give for a pill right about now so she wouldn't care what was happening. "No," she told herself. "I need to be here for the younger girls for as long as I can."

When Cece was finished, they made their way, hand-in-hand, back to the dressing room. The man had waited for them. "Shower time, girls. Follow me."

Lola approached the man. She shoved her finger at the man's chest. "What gives you the right? What gives you the right to take away our choices?" To Lola, death would be a better companion. She reached over onto the table and picked up a bottle of aerosol hairspray. Without thought or warning, she sprayed the liquid right in the man's eyes. He quickly squeezed his eyes shut, tears streaming down his face from the burn, and covered them with his hands.

"Get me some water," he yelled to one of the Latino women. She grabbed him by the arm and led him to the sink.

Lola wasn't finished yet. He was the only one there upon whom to take out her rage. She rushed the sink and knocked the man to the floor. He was at a disadvantage as he still couldn't see. She used all of her might to punch him square in the nose. She erupted at the thought of what they would do to the girls once they were purchased. Another punch. She erupted at her choices being taken away from her. Another punch. Blood began to drip down from the man's nose.

Just then two strong hands tore her from her seated position on the measurement man. She was spun forward and punched squarely in the stomach. She doubled over in pain. The fight left her then. She was resigned to the fact she couldn't escape. Another man grabbed her from behind and straightened her body. The man in front of her punched her again in the stomach. The punch knocked the wind from her chest; she couldn't breathe. She began to hyperventilate. She managed to say, "Please." The man stopped his assault on her stomach. He spoke Spanish to the woman standing there next to the sink, watching. The woman quickly disappeared and returned with a paper bag. Apparently, hyperventilating was something they were prepared for.

"Breathe into bag," the man told her, puffing out the bag and closing one end of it. He held it out to her. Without hesitation, Lola took the offered bag and began breathing into it. Slowly, her breathing evened out. Her eyes widened as she wondered what would be done with her now. She flew into such a rage, she was able to take down a man just as tall, with equal muscle mass as her. She had done a number on him. *What would the fat man say when he saw the measurement man?*

Lola's face was ashen and pale. Her hands felt clammy. She hugged herself tight. She was deathly afraid at what would be done to her now. To her amazement, the man whom she had punched stood. He was presented with a clean, dry cloth. He held it to his nose. He looked at Lola with evil intent and said, "This way, ladies."

Not to be further delayed, the measurement man kept the cloth pressed to his nose and led the girls through a door in the back corner of the room. They entered another large room with numerous shower heads and half-tiled walls separating each shower. Each stall had shampoo, conditioner, and soap.

This would be Lola's first shower in ten days. She hoped the hot water would take some of her pain away. All of her muscles were bunched into cords. In the middle of the room sat two rows of long benches. She stopped at an empty spot and reached for the hem of her dress. It degraded and humiliated her that the men with assault rifles were standing in the shower room with the girls, but she needed a shower. She would try to relish the feel of hot water raining down on her skin. She lifted the hem of her dress over her head and placed the discarded dress on the bench. Hopefully, she wouldn't have to put it back on anytime soon. She made her way to an empty stall and turned on the faucet. The handle only moved one way: up. She pushed the handle up and lukewarm spray assaulted her body. This was not the hot shower she had imagined. Still she lingered. She could clean herself, and that was all that mattered.

She took her time washing and conditioning her hair. Then she started to wash her body. From her peripheral vision, she could see the guards openly gawking at the girls, but their most intense stares were turned on her. She felt them burn holes through her body. She made quick work of washing herself and stepped from the shower where one of the team of ladies was waiting with a fresh towel. She dried off and wrapped the towel securely around herself. Sitting on the bench, she waited for the last of the girls to finish.

"Leave your clothes. You won't need them anymore," the measurement man said as he herded the girls back through the door and into the dressing room. He took great care in choosing a dressing table for each girl. When that job was finished, he handed each girl her negligee for the evening. Lola was handed the white one she had worn the day the ugly, fat, bald man had touched her. A day she was thankful the drugs made her temporarily forget. Now she couldn't forget. Once she was dressed, she sat at the cushioned chair at the dressing table. A Latino woman came up to her and began straightening her hair with a blow dryer and a round hair brush. She had naturally straight hair, but she guessed they wanted it to shine tonight. While the woman was styling her hair, she looked at what some of the other girls were wearing. Dangani wore white, but Cece wore red and Alisha wore blue. White, she ventured, equaled virginity, but Dangani was raped. Did that not count? *Maybe they raped her orally? Why harm the merchandise?* She could only imagine an unspoiled girl brought more money.

Next, the woman went to work on her makeup. The woman contrasted the innocence of the white negligee with sultry eye makeup and just a hint of blush. Her lips were painted a candy apple red, which made her already full lips look much fuller. The short, bald, fat man came into the room to inspect his products. He approved of most of the girls, but not of

Dangani. "Get this girl another negligee. One that shows off the buds of her breasts," he ordered in Spanish. He turned to address the girls in the room. "Girls, it has been my pleasure keeping you for the last several days, but I have some very interested men who are willing to spend hundreds of thousands of dollars on you tonight. Because of that, I don't want anyone panicking, so I have brought your drugs. Be good girls and take your pills for Papi."

Each woman at the dressing table handed a girl a pill. Lola took the pill from the outstretched hand of her hair dresser and thankfully swallowed it. "We will wait thirty minutes so your pills have a chance to take effect. Then, it's off to the catwalk for each of you. Don't disappoint Papi," the ugly, bald, fat man said in a heavy Spanish accent.

Apparently, they were being called in order of their dressing tables. Lola's was last. She watched as the girls came back into the dressing room without a care in the world. She didn't care what was about to happen, as long as they kept giving her pills. Her turn came. The man with the gun motioned for her to rise. She rose and made her way to the catwalk.

STRONGER

Rob entered the room designated for his alias, Jim Ruffing. He noticed a floor-to-ceiling two-way mirror, a red leather chair, a coffee table, and telephone. He sat, uncomfortably, in the chair. He had to act like this wasn't bothering him, but the truth was, he was ready to kill everyone in the barn that evening, sellers and buyers alike. He couldn't stand the injustice of what he was about to do. He was there only to purchase Lola Sardeson. *But what about the other innocent girls?* Her father had supplied more than adequate funds and advised outbidding anyone who wanted her. Rob would purchase Lola tonight. Steve, Tony, and Aaron were also undercover as Jim Ruffing's security detail. Every buyer here had their own security.

The team and their boss had worked swiftly to establish a background able to withstand Ortiz's scrutiny and gain admittance to tonight's auction. They worked for two days straight, no one sleeping more than a total of two hours. The result? Rob had a spotless invitation to tonight's auction and had his team as well. He didn't want to have to look at the girls as they were paraded down the catwalk. That only infuriated him more. His lip curled in disgust at the thought of what was happening all around him. "Just buy her. Just buy her," he repeated over and over to himself.

He rubbed at his forearm in a soothing gesture. When the first girl approached the runway, he flinched and squeezed his eyes shut. He didn't want to take part in the abasement that was occurring this evening. Why he was the one undercover was a mystery to him. Why couldn't it be one of his brothers? He forced his eyes open. He couldn't miss Lola Sardeson. A pained expression pierced his face. It was a good thing no one could see inside the rooms.

One thought, one singular thought brought him comfort. It was this thought that made him clench and unclench his fists over and over again: He would shut down the Ortiz Cartel if it was the last thing he did. He was sickened at the fact he couldn't save every girl here tonight. He could only save Lola. Her father had supplied the picture, so Rob sat anxiously awaiting Lola.

The telephone in the room rang. "Hello?" Rob answered.

"Can I get you something to drink, sir? Before we begin with tonight's auction?" the voice responded.

He might as well play the part. "Scotch please," he cooed.

"Very well, sir."

A moment later there was a knock at the door. A beautiful Latino woman with long brown hair and deep brown eyes met him as he answered the door. She handed his drink to him. He took it and offered her a $100 tip. The woman smiled brightly at him, and he couldn't help but wonder how someone so beautiful ended up working here.

Before entering the private room, he was briefed on the symbolism of the colors the girls wore. White stood for virgin, red stood for previous exploits, and blue stood for one previous exploit, so the men could tell what tightness the girls were before purchasing them.

Going against his own rule, he took a long swallow of scotch. The girl in front of him couldn't be more than fourteen years old. He had no way of knowing who was bidding, as each room was as private as his. He did get a glimpse of the men prior to entering the room. Hor d'oeuvres and drinks were served in a very luxurious waiting area of the barn. He didn't know which man went to which room, so he would have no way of rescuing the girl that stumbled before him in heels that were obviously too high for her. She wore blue and still that fact did not deter the outrage he felt at the damage and helplessness of the evening. He finished his drink by the time the third girl paraded by. How he wasn't breaking down the doors of the rooms and putting a bullet into the men's heads was beyond him. He telephoned for another drink. This would be his last one. Two and he could still function should something go wrong. Two and he could still hit a target dead-on from two hundred yards away.

He counted. Twelve girls in all had been sent careening down the runway. They must be drugged, he thought to himself, because the girls he was looking at didn't look like they much minded being on that stage. They looked like they were zombies doing what they were ordered to do. *What had they suffered before tonight?*

His eyes just happened to be fixed on the door as the next girl emerged. She looked older than the rest. She could walk in the ridiculously high heels she wore. She had experience and yet she wore white. That intrigued him. Her facial expression was one of indifference. He would give anything to take it away from her. This girl was stirring his emotions. He felt for her. He wanted to save her, if no one else, from the misery that awaited her once she was purchased. He wondered then, how many of the men were sadistic animals? They had to be to purchase a person.

He could see the way her brows knitted together as she self-consciously looked at the mirrors reflecting back her image. He had to save her. If no one else, this one! He had to protect this frightened girl from the monsters bidding on her tonight. He was moved and touched by her. The way her long, blond hair fell over her large, natural breasts inspired him. His lips parted. He brought his fingers up to touch his lips, imagining her lips touching his. He licked his lips as if readying to kiss her. Her frightened blue eyes called to him the way no other eyes had. He felt guilt. He was attracted to her. He was moved by her. He felt emotions come over him; emotions he hadn't even felt for his Lizzie. How could he forget his Lizzie so easily? How could he let another woman affect him so? He remembered Lizzie's easy smile and beautiful eyes.

He tried to turn his head, but when he did he caught a glimpse of her hard ass, which was peeking out of the back of her nightie as she made her way past him. He was conflicted. His cock was thumping in his dress slacks. He brought his lips together in a slight grimace. He didn't want to feel for or be aroused by this woman. He reached up to massage and sooth his tense neck muscles. She had a killer body: toned and defined, yet soft in the right places, and she was a virgin. His cock pulsed again, this time straining against his pants. He hadn't ever been this attracted to a woman before. He had to do something. If he could just contact his brothers, they could tail her and whoever bought her; he could save her. But he was required to leave his cell phone outside the room in a box full of cell phones. He couldn't contact them. He was stuck in this box incredibly aroused, astonishingly touched, yet disturbed by his guilt.

"Fuck!" Rob reached for the phone. That was Lola! He had been so touched, so excited, he forgot what he was doing there. He barked out a number, "One hundred grand, American."

"I'm sorry, sir, but the bidding is already at two hundred and fifty American," a woman said with a Spanish accent.

"Three hundred American." He had to win this auction. He was given three hundred and fifty thousand dollars to buy her tonight. "Please, God, let me win," he repeated again and again. He couldn't remember praying since Lizzie's death. He had given up on God until this exact moment. He had to have her. He had to protect her. He had to win this auction.

"Sir, it's your bid. It's between you and one other man. You both seem to want her. The bid is three fifty, American."

Shit. Fuck. He was going to lose her. "Three seventy-five, American." Now Rob was dipping into his own money. He had to win. He had to have her. As guilty as that made him feel, he had to have Lola for himself.

"You've won the bid, sir. Number six has backed out. She is all yours." Those words, "all yours," made his cock twitch. What was he thinking? He had been so overcome with emotion and desire that he forgot about his Lizzie? Lola took his Lizzie away, and he didn't think he liked that. He couldn't have this girl. What would she see in him but a man who drank too much, took dangerous jobs, and had a death wish? He'd had his chance at the real thing, but it had been stolen from him.

He looked down at himself and felt immense guilt. He lowered his gaze to the plush carpet adorning the private room. He bit his lower lip at the thought of what Lola Sardeson was able to do to him. His chin began to quiver. *Lizzie.* His eyes tried to avoid looking at the raging hard-on he got at the thought of Lola's hard ass peeking out of her nightie. He imagined the way she would respond to him. *Could he have both? Could he keep his memories of Lizzie and still protect and allow feelings for Lola?* He was so confused. He shook his head. He had to get back into the mission. He had won the bid. He would be returning Lola to her father in two days. He already didn't want to let her go, and he didn't even know her. Now that he saw her, and had the reaction he did, he didn't want to let those feelings go. He felt alive for the first time since Lizzie's death.

After the auction, the men gathered in the large waiting room. Each girl was delivered to the correct number. Rob awaited his Lola. Shit, he was already thinking of her as his. He had to get a grip. Lola was brought to him wearing the same nightie she had been wearing on the catwalk.

"Don't you have something else she can put on?" Rob asked the man who delivered her.

"No, senor."

Rob removed his coat and wrapped it around Lola's trembling body. Of course she was scared. He just bought her, and she had no idea who he was or his real purpose.

Lola straightened at his touch. Her back went rigid, and her toned, defined arms pressed against her sides. She allowed him to wrap the coat around her, but she didn't make eye contact. Instead, her eyes darted around the room, taking in the sight of the young girls with the nasty, filthy men who purchased them. She spotted Dangani and her heart sank. A knot formed in her stomach. What would the man who had Dangani gripped by the arm do with such a young girl? A pained expression crossed Lola's face. She spotted Alisha with a younger man. Lola wondered how much the man had paid for Alisha. She couldn't find Cece no matter how much she tried. She chastised herself for not fighting harder. The whole situation was hopeless. She had just been purchased herself. She was of no use to Alisha, Dangani, or Cece now. Slowly, Lola put distance between herself and Rob, and to her surprise, he let her.

Lola prided herself on being strong, but she couldn't stop the tears from forming in her eyes. She blinked several times to keep them from falling. She wouldn't let the man who had just purchased her see her as weak.

Rob could smell his favorite flower. Moving in closer to Lola, he confirmed it. She smelled of honeysuckle. He inhaled her sweet scent deeply into his lungs and let out an exasperated sigh. She cringed and backed away from him upon his exhale. *Did he have bad breath?* She was shaking violently now. Whatever drug they had given the girls must be starting to wear off. The only thing he could think his breath would smell like is the mint chewing gum and the scotch he had. *What upset her so at the sight or smell of him?*

He placed his large, callused hand to the small of her back and led her outside the barn. He looked for his brothers and found them standing in the same spot he had left them. Seeing Rob with Lola, the three men approached. Rob continued to guide Lola to the SUV. He opened the back door for her, and she scrambled inside and pressed herself against the far door. He crawled in after her and sat in the middle, making way for Aaron.

Their legs brushed and Rob felt an energy travel through his body like he had never known. She must have felt something too because she jumped and made the cutest hiccup sound. The warmth from her leg spread throughout his body. He felt a pulling in his groin. He was reacting to this woman. His eyes were focused on a point on the back of the front seat. He was concentrating on not ripping her clothes, if one could call them that, right from her body. He didn't want to frighten her, so he stared straight ahead. His brows knitted together in concentration.

"You alright, man? You look like you're about to blow a gasket." Aaron patted Rob on the shoulder.

"Yeah, I just will never get the image of those young girls out of my mind." He didn't lie, that was bothering him. Hearing his words, Lola jerked her head to look into his eyes. Blue met bright gray, and they held each other. Rob read the look of understanding in Lola's eyes. He had to tell her the truth. But when was a good time to tell someone she was owned. They needed to clear the farm first, just to be on the safe side.

STRONGER

CHAPTER ELEVEN

"Go. Stop Number Eight. His payment didn't go through. Bring back the girl. We will sell her to Number Six," Ortiz ordered his three men armed with AR type 223 rifles. The men rushed out of the back door of the barn. They spotted Rob and his brothers as they were placing Lola into the backseat of their SUV. The men ran toward the SUV, but it started to drive away before they could catch it. They knew Ortiz would kill them if they didn't retrieve the girl. If they failed their assigned task, they would each receive one bullet to the head, execution style. They doubled back and hopped into their SUV. The driver barreled after Rob and Lola.

The ride to the airport was torture. Lola's leg brushed up against Rob's every time they hit a pot hole, sending jolts of energy through his body and to his groin. Mexico did not have the best roads. They had all of the travel documents needed in a bag in the backseat because failure tonight was not an option. Steve would have to fly the plane. They couldn't very well walk in with a half-dressed Lola. "My Lola," he growled under his breath.

Just then, Rob was pulled out of his thoughts by the unmistakable sound of gunfire. AR223 if he recalled correctly from his training. *He wasn't driving. Shit.* He would prefer to be driving, to be in control, but he and Steve had the same driver's training on outmaneuvering another vehicle. They had both been taught to drive defensively yet aggressively. Steve was doing a good job of maneuvering the big vehicle through the light traffic on the back roads.

The Cartel's SUV wasn't far behind. Each time the Cartel got close enough, they fired.

"Get down and stay down," Rob ordered as he pushed Lola's head between her knees. The sound of glass splintering into a million tiny pieces filled his hears. The Cartel's bullet had connected with the back window. *Even better,* Rob thought. He pulled out his side arm, a SIG 226, and shot out the back window completely. Now he could engage the Cartel. He fired several rounds through the now windowless back. He aimed unsuccessfully for the driver.

Bang! Bang! Bang! The sound was loud, and Lola covered her ears. With each shot, Lola jerked. She had never been exposed to anything, let alone a gun fight in a moving vehicle. Her chest caved inward and brought her body closer to her knees. She was flexible and had no problems tucking her head tightly between her knees. However, her body was trembling. *Why were there people shooting at them? He bought her. What was going on?*

Rob brought the gun up and aimed it at the driver. The holes in these back roads were preventing him from getting off a good shot. He fired, but it went wide and to the right as the SUV bumped along the road. He brought his side arm up again. "Keep it steady, will you?"

"I'm trying, but these roads are a mess." Steve sped up and tried to outrun the Cartel. He came into a small town and made a hard left onto a side street. The SUV made the turn, but Steve overcorrected and wasted time by having to reverse before he could pull straight. He made quick work of correcting the trajectory of the vehicle, and his speed reached ninety miles an hour in no time. They didn't, however, lose the Cartel. They were gaining on Lola and the men. Steve made a hard right into an alleyway.

"Shit. It's a dead end. We're going to have to hold them off," Steve yelled out, as he brought the car to a stop. The Cartel's SUV careened into the same alleyway and slowed to a crawl about one hundred feet behind The Unit's SUV.

"Get on the floor," Rob ordered a trembling Lola. Lola obeyed and got on the floor of the vehicle, making her body as small as possible. Lola hid her face as she lay on the floor of the SUV. She began crying, fear and adrenaline coursing through her body.

The men got out of the SUV and stood behind open doors with guns aimed at the Cartel. The Cartel opened fire. Bullets zinged and whizzed by the men's heads. The men were experienced in warfare and had no trouble keeping up with the fight. They fired back. The Cartel was out-trained and outgunned. They had three men; Rob had four, including himself. Rob didn't understand why the men were after Lola, but there was no way they were getting her back. Rob aimed at the driver's side window of the cartel's SUV. *Bang!* A carefully placed bullet landed right between the eyes of the man standing behind the door. Rob saw his body slump to the ground.

Whiz! Thump! This time a bullet hit Steve. He staggered back into the vehicle grasping the wound. He lay back against the seat holding his right shoulder.

"Where are you hit, man?" Rob yelled over the gunfire.

"My shoulder. I'll be fine." Steve struggled, powering through the pain, back to his fighting position behind the car door. He only needed a moment to regain his composure. It sure hurt like a bitch.

They were going to have to draw the men out from behind their doors. And Lola would have to be the bait. *Should he risk it? Would she ever forgive him?*

"We have what you want!" Rob yelled to the men in the other vehicle.

"Send her out. We only want her."

An easily transparent lie, Rob thought. "We need to see you're serious. Lay down your weapons, and I will send her out."

"No way! Send her out, and we call it a night."

Rob leaned into the vehicle and brought his lips close to Lola's ear, inhaling his favorite scent. "Don't worry. We will kill them before they have a chance to touch you again."

"How much am I worth to you? How much did you spend on me?" Lola spat the words at Rob. Rob longed to tell her the whole truth, but now was not the time. He needed her to lure the men out from behind their car. He knew they wouldn't kill her; she was too valuable to them.

"Listen, I don't know if you can do this, but when the man comes to you, I need to you knee him in the balls as hard as you can. I need you to make him drop to the ground," Rob pleaded into Lola's ear. Lola looked up at him in confusion. He wanted her help? He seemed to realize she was conflicted, "Please. Just trust me. I'll explain everything as soon as I can. Now, do you think you can do this?"

"My pleasure," Lola grinned. Finally, she could take out the rage she had been feeling on a person who deserved it.

"Get up and slowly walk towards the other vehicle," Rob motioned to Lola with his gun. He really didn't like the look of fear in her eyes as she looked at him, nor did he like sending her into the direct line of fire, but he really didn't have a choice if he was going to end this and keep Lola safe.

Lola stood on shaky legs. Rob ran a hand up and down her back, trying to soothe her, but it wasn't working. At his touch, she cringed and moved away. *How was he going to make her want him after this stunt?* Lola moved slowly, one foot in front of the other, stumbling, to the space between the two vehicles. Rob and his men stayed behind the doors. Lola had traveled about thirty feet when a man from the other vehicle came out and grabbed her roughly by the arm as he tried to hurry her along. But she remembered her mission, so she struggled and pulled against the man. He turned to face her, to tell her to move quickly, and when he did, she brought her right foot down hard on his left foot. Before he recovered from the pain, she drove her knee up and connected with his groin, sending the man to the ground curled up in the fetal position.

Thank God she was able to pull it off, Rob thought, because it caused the last man to leave the cover of his vehicle. As soon as he stepped a foot from behind the vehicle, Rob aimed and fired, another between-the-eyes shot. Two for two tonight. He would call this a good night.

Seeing her chance, Lola took off running—to where she didn't know, but she had to escape. Rob ran after her before she had a chance to escape into the dark night of some shanty Mexican town. He ran with all of his might. She was fast, but he managed to grab her by the arm.

"You have to come with us. We will protect you."

"Is that what you call it? I thought I did a rather fine job of protecting myself."

Rob smiled. "You did. I wasn't sure you could pull it off."

"You don't know me. I spend a lot of time at the gym training. Daddy's orders," she said as the adrenaline began to leave her body.

She slumped into Rob. Rob could feel her muscles, her soft breasts, pressed up against his hard chest. He didn't back away from her. He placed his rough, calloused hands on the soft skin of her arms.

But as soon as she caught a whiff of his breath, she immediately cringed and backed away from him. *Why was she distancing herself?* Their connection had him humming. He was sure she felt it, too. It was too strong, too base, too electric not to feel.

Aaron and Tony loaded the dead Cartel bodies into their SUV and reversed it out of the alleyway while Rob fixed up Steve's shoulder. Thank God people minded their own business in Mexico. He knew interfering in the many drug gangs that littered the land could get one killed.

Rob's former title in the Army was Special Forces Medical Sergeant. That meant he had a lot of practice treating emergency and trauma patients in the field during his five tours in Afghanistan. He was thankful for his expert knowledge set. For tonight, he needed to do a quick bandage job on Steve, just enough to stop the bleeding. He would stitch him up when they got back to the plane.

Steve was out of commission, and Rob didn't want to leave Lola's side. How did he convince her he was the good guy when he still carried the guilt of not saving his Lizzie? There it was, his Lizzie.

Somehow, he had to convince himself he could protect Lola before he ever entertained the thought of being with her. Sure, being around her did something to him—something no one, not even his Lizzie, could do. He felt her—her presence, her being, at the very heart of his. The first step towards connecting with Lola was to show her he was the good guy. That he didn't come there to own her per se, although she would be his. More than anything, he didn't want her to be afraid of him. He felt a connection not even thoughts of Lizzie could stop. He had to explore it, if just to see if she felt it, too. He didn't know how he was going to accomplish that and hold onto Lizzie at the same time, but he had to try. This connection he felt for Lola was powerful, heady, soul-altering.

Aaron parked next to the private jet, and for the first time that night, Rob heard Lola's voice, soft and soothing. "Where are you taking me? What do you plan on doing with me? How much did you pay for me?" she asked in almost a whisper.

She had no idea why the last question was so important to her, except she rationalized the more money he spent on her, the better care he would take of her.

Rob let her questions go unanswered.

"Where are you taking me?" Lola asked again, looking at Rob with a sadness that was breaking his heart.

"Home," he said, unable to keep the secret any longer. Her eyes widened in disbelief. She met his gaze for the second time that night. He reached out and grabbed her hand. The same energy that attacked him in the car was causing a tingling sensation to spread down his spine. "Let's get you on board. You don't need to fear me. I would never hurt you." With a firm grasp of her hand, he led her to the steps of the airplane.

CHAPTER
TWELVE

Rob made sure Lola was seated in one of the comfortable chairs which surrounded a small table. He reached down and grabbed ahold of the seatbelt strap, buckling her into her seat. "Can I get you something to drink?" Rob knew she was twenty, not quite old enough to drink, but, he rationalized, she had a rough few weeks. The nagging thought of whether or not he was good enough for Lola entered his mind. She came from a wealthy home. Sure, he made good money taking high-risk jobs, but it was nothing compared to the lifestyle her father led.

"Don't worry. I will be twenty-one in two months," Lola reassured Rob before he approached the bar.

"What would you like to drink?"

"A vodka and tonic, please."

"I won't stop you, not after what you've been through." He walked over to the small bar, which adorned the right corner of the jet, placed four ice cubes in the glass, poured a healthy dose of vodka and a splash of tonic into the glass. He returned and handed it to her. He watched, mesmerized, as she brought the glass to her full, red, kissable, soft lips and parted them. She tilted her head back slightly, and he watched as she swallowed the drink. Just the sight enthralled him. Her perfectly tanned skin, the way her neck muscles moved to swallow the drink. He could picture those luscious lips wrapped around his cock. He longed to place his hand against her throat while she swallowed his seed, to feel her swallow all of him down into herself.

It was like she could feel his eyes on her, and she wanted to keep them there. She looked up at him through her eyelashes coyly. He was a very attractive man. He wasn't much older than she. It was his devastating eyes that did her in. He was haunted in a way that called to her. His eyes were so expressive. She could tell this man had seen his share of pain. His smoldering gray eyes watched her. She could feel a pull unlike any she had ever felt. She knew she was attractive, but she didn't think a man of his caliber, who looked like he did, who rescued her and was taking her home, would feel the same about a twenty-year-old princess who led a very sheltered life. This was a man who had seen the world, good and bad. The worst thing she had ever experienced up until her kidnapping was maxing out one of her daddy's credit cards and going through the embarrassment of it being declined.

Rob moved past her to get to the window seat. He sat down and buckled his seatbelt. The plane would be departing any minute. It couldn't take off fast enough for him. He didn't want any more trouble from the

Ortiz Cartel. Not when he was so close to completing the mission.

"Why are you taking me home?" Lola asked, afraid of the answer.

"We," Rob gestured to the other men sitting across from him already beginning to doze off to sleep, "work for Blackrain Security. We handle jobs the government can't or won't. Your father hired us to rescue you. So when I say you are going home, I mean you are going home to your father."

"What about the others? What about Dangani?" Lola asked as she looked down at her hands resting in her lap. She wanted to see them, to make sure they were okay. "Why didn't you save them?"

"We were hired by your father to rescue you. You were the mission. Please believe me, I wanted to take out every motherfucker there, but I couldn't risk you."

"What will happen to them now? Will anyone even try to find them?"

"They're gone, Lola. You have to let them go."

"You don't understand," Lola said, raising her voice an octave, "they are so young, so innocent."

"I understand. Please believe me. It took everything in me not to shoot every man there tonight. I am sick with the thought of what is happening to them."

Rocking back and forth in her seat, she whispered, "Me too."

Lola became quieter, less animated than he had ever seen her. Trying anything he could to calm her, he reached over and touched her knee. "Your father is waiting to see you. He has been worried sick about you. You have to think about that. You can't think about the others. You have to let them go."

She didn't want to let them go. She didn't want to forget them. Swallowing hard, she did the only thing she could and vowed to pray for them every night and to never forget them. Rubbing the pain from her chest with her palm, she realized she didn't even know their last names, so she couldn't locate their families. The situation was hopeless. Lola's shoulders slumped forward as silent tears streamed down her face. What choice did she have? Her father had money. Of course, he would pay to have his princess tracked down and rescued. Still, the thought of what the other girls were enduring made the tears fall harder, faster. She recognized that Rob was right. She would have to let them go. But nothing could stop her from praying for them every night and remembering them every day. She would talk to her father about organizing a foundation to stop sex-slave trafficking. And she would play an active role in stopping the human trafficking whether he approved or not.

Gathering her courage, Lola raised her chin and met Rob's steel gray eyes. "I want to see my father. I want him to know that I'm alright. I don't want him worried any longer than he has to be, but I don't want to go home with him." She sighed. If she went back to her father, he would never let his princess leave her tower again. "I can't live with him again," she pleaded. "After I get a chance to console him, can't you take me back to my Cambridge home? I finally have my own life, and I want to keep it that way."

"We can discuss that once we get back to Blackrain. From what I know about your father, he isn't just going to let you go. He is going to expect you to have some kind of security detail. Especially after he hears how the Cartel came after us."

Rob wondered why the Cartel *had* come after them. He entered the correct account number for the wire transfer. He even entered his own account number to make up for the extra twenty-five grand it took to buy her. Maybe the Cartel got ahold of his name during the transfer and figured out he wasn't Jim Ruffing? Still, if they got their money, what should they care that she was gone. Unless, the account numbers were dummies and her father never had any intention of paying that kind of money to rescue his daughter? He would find out when he got back to the office.

"Can I ask you a very personal question, Ms. Sardeson?"

"Please, call me Lola."

"Okay, Lola. Can I ask you a question? There's something that's been bothering me all night…."

"Sure."

"When I touched you earlier and was in your personal space, you cringed. As if you couldn't stand being comforted by me. Did they do something to you while you were held captive?"

Should she tell him what the man had done to her? No one knew, and she could keep it that way if she wanted. No one had to know. Still, she felt compelled into nothing but strict honesty when she looked into his smoky gray eyes.

"Mr. Ortiz, that's how everybody referred to him, touched me inappropriately. He didn't rape me, but I still feel violated."

Lola heard a low growl come from Rob before he bolted straight out of his seat. His hands were shaking, his body trembling. He paced up and down the aisle, running his hand roughly over his face. "He's dead," Lola heard him mumble. "He's dead!" He repeated it over and over again as he paced back and forth.

All Rob could feel was the pounding of his heart in his chest. He opened and closed his fists, trying to move the blood back into his hands. His breath was coming in short, ragged surges. He heard himself mumbling. He could only picture the most brutal death for Mr. Ortiz. He pictured slicing him from throat to gut with a very sharp knife. He pictured his guts being disemboweled from his body. He pictured the man begging for his life while his guts lay on the outside of his body. He wanted him to beg for his life to no avail. He wanted to be the one to cause him excruciating pain.

Then he felt her standing behind him. She brought her soft, petite hand up and rested it upon his shoulder. Immediately, he stopped shaking. His heart rate slowed to a dull thud. With one touch, she had calmed him. He turned to look at her, and she lowered her hand to her side. He gazed at her piercing electric blue eyes, straight to her core. *Was it possible she felt the same connection he felt?*

She lifted her hand again and stepped closer to him, invading his personal space. She raised her hand and gently traced his tattoo under the sleeve of his t-shirt with her fingertips. She didn't know what was making her so bold with a man she didn't know. At the clubs, she would never touch a man with her hands or her lips. Those two areas were strictly forbidden. Her fingers finished trailing the swirl on his arm and dropped back to her side. His breathing had slowed.

"Can we sit back down?" she asked in a gentle voice. Rob didn't answer but moved back to his seat.

"You didn't cringe from me that time. Why did you before? I was just trying to comfort you much the same way you just calmed me down." Although that was the understatement of the year. No one—God forgive him, not even his Lizzie—could calm him with just a touch. One touch from Lola and his world was right. He was the man he always wanted to be. Gone were his past mistakes. He had protected her from the Ortiz Cartel. That had to, in some way, make up for what he let happen to his Lizzie.

"To be honest, it was the alcohol on your breath. Mr. Ortiz smelled the same way when he was touching me. So the smell brought back the memories," she confessed, unsure why she felt the need tell him the truth.

"But you drink alcohol," he retorted, desperate to understand. "Is it all alcohol or just a certain type?"

"Whatever it was you were drinking. That's what triggered the memory."

"Scotch," he mumbled to himself. Lola looked at him with passion in her eyes. She felt their connection, too. He was sure of it. She just didn't know how deeply he felt it.

He made a promise to God right then and there. If God would see fit to allow Lola to be his, his to own, then he would never drink another drop of scotch as long as he lived. He had to own her though. The thought of another man near her sent him into a rage. And if he were to ever witness such a thing, he would surely be spending his remaining days in a prison cell. It was one thing for him to kill a man on a mission, quite another to kill one in cold blood. He wasn't a murderer, although some would call him that after all of the lives he took in Afghanistan and on missions with his current employer, but never once did he kill in cold blood. Lola brought it out of him. He would kill for her, and he didn't even know if she would kiss him.

"Why do you think the men came after us?" Lola asked.

"I have been trying to figure that one out myself. The only thing I can think of is they didn't get their money."

"That's just like him," Lola huffed.

"What do you mean?"

"How much did you pay for me?"

"Three hundred seventy-five thousand dollars." Lola choked on her drink. She spit some of it back out of her mouth and into her glass.

"You're kidding? There is no way my father would part with that much money. He would rescue me, which is what he did by hiring you, but he would never turn over that much money."

Rob didn't want her to know he spent $25,000 of his own money. "So he did pull his money before the transfer was finalized. I won't lie to you, Lola, this is not good. The Cartel consider you their property, and if they had a bid of $375,000, they aren't just going to let you walk away."

"What am I going to do?" A shudder visibly moved through her at the thought. "I can't go back to Daddy's. I want out from under his thumb. He dictates who I can and cannot see, who I have to be friends with, where I have to shop, where I can and cannot go. I can't live like that anymore." She lowered her head into her hands and began to softly cry. She didn't want to go back, but she wasn't safe on her own.

"I can stay with you," Rob offered before he even thought about what that would mean. "I can protect you." What if she didn't feel the same connection? Could he really protect her while she was out with another guy? He just wouldn't let her get close to another guy. He had a new mission: to make Lola his.

STRONGER

Lola sat in the SUV with Rob right next to her on the way back to Blackrain's office. She was very conscious of where Rob's leg was because it kept brushing against hers. Each touch would heat her stomach and make her feel longing deep in her core. She felt butterflies at just the sight of Rob. She had never experienced anything close to this before. Sure she had guys rubbing up against her when she danced, but never in her life had she ever felt this emptiness mixed with fluttering in the pit of her stomach, this longing for a man to be inside her, filling her up, like she felt for Rob.

They pulled in front of a small, non-descript, two-story brick building that housed Blackrain Security. High-tech security cameras followed them. The inside was much like she expected. The downstairs had a few fake plants in a few corners and there were cubes that each held desks. She walked past the kitchenette on her way to the stairs. The kitchen contained a small table and three chairs, a microwave, a stove and oven, a refrigerator, and a coffee pot. It was a complete setup. The staircase was on the outside of the wall and led to a closed glass door. She imagined the upstairs was where they held their meetings. She didn't see any conference tables in amongst the cubes. They made their way up the metal staircase and entered through the glass door. The upstairs was much more modern, with Impressionist paintings adorning the walls. Again, she saw the same fake plants she saw downstairs. Someone liked their greenery.

Rob stopped outside of another door, this one frosted glass. The name on the door read 'Tyrrell Greenwood.' Rob knocked twice and heard, "Come in."

Rob placed his hand on the small of Lola's back and led her into the office. Lola's father was seated at the large conference table. He stood and rushed to hug her. She hugged him back with all her might. She was happy to see the relieved look in his eyes. As soon as they finished with the embrace, Mr. Sardeson stepped back to look at his daughter. She was still wearing the white negligee and coat from the previous day.

"Can someone get her some clothes for Christ's sake?" Mr. Sardeson bellowed through the office.

"Of course, sir. Aaron, please get Ms. Sardeson some clothes from the locker room." Tyrrell motioned for Aaron to move quickly.

Rob found Mr. Sardeson in three long strides. He grabbed the man by the collar of his expensive suit and bunched it up at the neck. "How could you?" Rob spat into his face. He was so close to Mr. Sardeson he felt the huffed breath from the man on his face.

"What are you talking about?" Mr. Sardeson accused, acting tougher than he felt.

"You could have gotten her killed. All over money!" Rob yelled. "They came after us. Your guy, who pulled the money, didn't wait long enough. You know what? Forever won't be long enough. They want her. She is worth three hundred and seventy five grand to them. You think they are just going to let her walk away?"

"I only provided three hundred and fifty thousand. Where did the other money come from?" That was Mr. Sardeson's only question.

"That's not your concern," Rob responded. He really didn't want Lola to know he put up the remaining amount.

"Wait just a second. What do you mean he pulled the money?" Tyrrell asked, looking to Rob.

"He gave us about a twenty-minute window from the time the auction closed to the time he pulled his money. Thank God we were already in the SUV when Ortiz's men started after us. We barely made it back alive. We had a good, old-fashioned shoot-out in the streets of some Mexican town." Rob looked directly at Mr. Sardeson. So much for Lola's father liking him.

"Mr. Sardeson, is this true? Did you pull your funds?" Tyrrell asked, moving to pry Rob's hand from his expensive collar.

"There was no way I was paying some criminal for the return of my own daughter. That is what I hired you to do. And I see I made the wise choice."

"Mr. Sardeson," Tyrrell said in his most patronizing voice, "Rob is right. They consider Lola their property. They are going to come after her."

"I plan on having her back under my protection this afternoon. She will no longer be attending Harvard. She will have around the clock body guards—"

"I'm not going back with you, Daddy," Lola interrupted in a low-pitched voice. "I will continue to go to Harvard. I will continue to have my own life." She raised her chin and met her father's calculating eyes. She stood solidly, waiting for his tirade. Surely, he wouldn't cause a scene in front of people. Nevertheless, she stood rooted to her spot, spine straight, eyes focused on her father's.

"You, young lady, will be coming home with me."

"I will not. I will find my own protection."

"With what means? I will cut you off so fast…"

Inhaling deeply through her nose, she responded, "Good. I'll use what I have in my trust fund. I'll find a job like everyone else. I don't want you to hate me, Daddy. I just want to have my own life. I'm tired of you controlling me."

"And how are you going to afford protection? You need me." He was looking straight into her eyes, begging her to defy him. "Around the clock protection isn't cheap. It will eat through your trust fund in a couple of months."

"I will be her protection, sir." Rob moved to stand beside Lola.

"See, Daddy. It's settled. Rob will protect me."

"I forbid it."

"You don't have a say, sir." Rob's eyes met dark, menacing ones. "Your daughter is an adult. If she doesn't want to go home with you, she doesn't have to. But rest assured, I will die before I let anything happen to her."

"Lola," Mr. Sardeson said, resorting to begging.

"I'm sorry, Daddy, but my mind is made up."

"If I provide funding for this protection, can we make sure he has backup?" Mr. Sardeson could never refuse his daughter anything. It was his fault she was still in danger.

"We can work something out." Tyrrell looked at Rob. "Care to tell me where the additional funds came from?"

"I'd rather not," Rob responded.

"That wasn't really a question."

"Fine. I put in the twenty-five grand, or we would have lost the auction," Rob said, lowering his head, embarrassed.

Lola's mouth dropped open. "Why?" she whispered.

"I couldn't lose you," Rob said, looking into her beautiful sea-foam colored eyes. All of the men in the room exchanged glances. *What did he mean?*

"I will pay you back," Mr. Sardeson said, reaching into his breast pocket and removing his checkbook.

"Lola, do you mind if I talk to my boss and your father for a minute, alone?" Rob asked, aware that damage had been done, aware that he had revealed too much.

"Perfect timing. Aaron, will you show Ms. Sardeson to the ladies' room so she can change?" Tyrrell asked.

Aaron opened the door for Lola, and she followed him down the hall. When Rob could no longer hear footsteps, he spoke. "I do not want my money back. I don't want payment for this job. I'm protecting her because I want to. If you want to pay the company for the other men's involvement, that's fine, but I will not take a penny of your money." He looked at Tyrrell, and Tyrrell knew he was serious.

"If you aren't doing this for the money, son, then why are you doing this?" Mr. Sardeson asked, cutting through the bullshit.

"I care for your daughter. Nothing will happen to her. No one will touch her, not as long as I am around. That's all you need to know."

"Tyrrell, I guess that leaves you and me to talk business," Mr. Sardeson said, dismissing Rob and turning his attention back to Tyrrell.

Rob waited outside the ladies' restroom for Lola. He wanted to be the one to tell her the good news. She would get what she wanted. She could go back to Harvard. But he also had to explain his new role in her life. She exited the bathroom dressed in men's jeans at least two sizes too big for her and a man's plain white V-neck undershirt. She had to keep a hand on the pants or they would fall down.

"Thanks for that. With my father. No one has ever stood up to him for me before."

"You don't have to thank me. You deserve to live your own life. I do need to talk to you though," Rob said, trying hard to avoid looking at her perky breasts covered by the thin fabric.

"Sure," she said, joining him in his walk down the hallway.

When they reached his cube, he pulled out his chair and offered her a seat.

"Thank you."

Rob leaned against his desk and crossed his arms over his chest. "Listen, I know we just met, but this detail I signed up for means you and I live together—twenty-four seven. You are never out of my sight."

"What about classes?" she inquired, anxious to get some resemblance of her old life back.

"I will escort you to your classes, and I will be waiting for you when you leave."

"What about your life?"

"Until this is over, you are my life."

"What about your girlfriend?" Surely he had to have a girlfriend, a man as gorgeous as he was. She let her eyes wander down his toned neck, over his Adam's apple, down to his broad, muscular chest. Her eyes traveled further still, subconsciously, down to his narrow hips and his strong, powerful legs to the tips of his work boots. She liked everything she saw. She took her time working her eyes back up his body while she waited for his response.

He felt it. He felt her eyes as if they were a soft caress. Her gaze pierced his body and heated him. His groin pulled. She wanted him. His heart actually fluttered in his chest. She made her appreciation of his body known. He liked that. She was bold and brave. He admired that about her. She was also honest. He thought about it and realized he had been completely honest with her about everything. Even with how he was feeling, although under the guise of protecting her. He told her she was his life, and he meant it.

"I don't have a girlfriend," he said, suddenly feeling sad. His thoughts were turning back to Lizzie. He started to feel the guilt of forgetting his Lizzie for as long as he had. Lola had taken his mind and cleared it of everything but her. How could he forget the love of his life? Could he ever forgive himself for forgetting her? Whatever this pull Lola had over him was, he would have to fight it. She was his mission. He would protect her because, if he was being honest with himself, he cared about her. She affected him, relieved his scarred mind. But he would never forget his Lizzie again. She deserved better than that.

"Oh," she said in surprise.

Rob escorted Lola back to her brownstone and parked on the street outside the front of her home. He admired the luxurious home in a refined area of Cambridge. He put his hand on her knee and held it in place indicating for her to stay in the car. She felt his piercing eyes look through her. She knew then she would never be able to hide anything from this man.

As Rob rounded the car, he admired her home. The wide steps led to a double door with large windows. The remaining wood had been painted black. He opened Lola's door and held out his hand to her. She took his hand and immediately electricity moved through his body. He shook his head—Lizzie. He chastised himself for feeling something. The only person he should be feeling something for is Lizzie. He warred with himself. He had to possess Lola. He had to keep her safe and convince her that he was a good man—a man she could be with. Holding her hand tightly, he helped her out of the vehicle. He looked around, on guard against the dangers that awaited her. When he deemed it safe, he led her by her hand up the stairs to her house.

"I have to get the key." She reached down under the mat and pulled out her key.

"You've got to be kidding me," Rob scoffed at her clichéd hiding place.

"What? No one knows it's here."

"Are you kidding me? That's the first place people look," he admonished her.

Her face flushed and heated under his look of disapproval. *What was it about him that made her want to please him in all things, even something so small as where she kept her key?*

Rob shook his head as Lola unlocked the door. She had one lock on the outside of the door which, to her credit, was a deadbolt. One would think her father would want more security for his daughter after the temper tantrum he had thrown today.

She unlocked the deadbolt, opened the double door, and they stepped inside to the vestibule. She used the key to unlock the second deadbolt on the hardwood double door, which protected her home from the outside world. She pushed her shoes, which were two sizes too big for her, off of her feet and placed them in the closet in the vestibule. She looked at Rob.

"Sorry, but we may need to move. My shoes stay on my feet. And as soon as we are inside, you are putting on a pair yourself." He smiled to please her. She nodded, understanding he was just trying to stay prepared. They stepped through the second set of doors into one of the most luxurious homes Rob had ever seen. Her daddy was definitely paying for this, or she had money of her own.

"Are you renting?" he inquired, curious as to her financial state.

"No. Daddy insisted he purchase it for me if I was going to live here in Cambridge."

He was immediately taken in by the earth tones, which adorned the walls, and the plush carpet that matched exactly. The floor plan was an open one. Standing in her living room, he could see a working fireplace, which embellished the right wall before the staircase. Her lush furniture was perfectly positioned in her living room, creating a classic space for entertaining. She had a coffee table in the middle of a couch, a love seat, and a recliner. He wondered which seat was her favorite. He noticed she did not have a television in her living room. Odd. That's when he turned his head and looked to the left wall where she had four bookshelves filled with books that appeared to have been read over and over again judging by the worn and cracked spines.

"No TV?"

"I like to read." She looked adoringly at her makeshift library. One day she would have a real library. But for now, these shelves that housed her favorite escapes would have to do.

Beyond the bookshelves and past the living room was her dining area. She had leather padded chairs surrounding a glass table top. As Rob moved closer, he could see the intricate leaf pattern that served as the base of the table. He admired the look. Everything went together in her home.

"Did you decorate yourself?"

"Yes. I insisted. Daddy wanted to hire someone, but I refused. As you can imagine, he wasn't happy about that."

"I like your place. It has a homey, calm feel to it."

"Thank you," she said as her cheeks flushed for the second time that morning.

Finally, at the back of the home, was her kitchen. It was filled with state-of-the-art appliances all in stainless steel, giving it a professional quality. It wasn't a large kitchen, but it was high-end. Rob could tell, remembering when he priced appliances to redo his kitchen.

Lizzie. The way they had spent time painstakingly decorating their home together. The fun they had at Home Depot picking out appliances and cabinetry. Her laugh. He bowed his head as the memory hit him. He rocked back on his feet and shoved his hands into his pockets.

"What's wrong?" Lola asked, noticing his change in demeanor.

"Just thinking."

"You look like you just lost your best friend," she said as she approached him cautiously. She now stood in his personal space. The air around her crackled to life with energy and electricity. She could feel the tension, the energy between them. She wanted to calm him. She wanted to please him. She wanted to remove that sad, hopeless look from his face. She touched his arm and he jumped. He was brought from his misery back into the light. His eyes met hers, and he stared unabashedly. She felt the heat, the fire, of his stare. She ran her hand lovingly down his arm towards his hand, which was still in his pocket. When she reached it, she tugged it free and took it in hers. She didn't know what came over her, but she brought his hand up to her mouth and placed a gentle, soft kiss, brushing her lips over the skin on the back of his hand. He instinctually stepped closer to her. She took his hand and used it to caress her face. She rubbed the backside of his hand over her cheek.

"Don't," he cautioned. "I'm broken."

"It's okay. I don't mean to fix you," she said as she brought his hand back down to his side and held it in hers.

"I need to look around. See what I need to keep you safe." He had to escape her presence. He felt the tension, the energy, the electricity between them so thick, he didn't know how he resisted not taking her in his arms and kissing her until she forgot everything but him. But he could not betray Lizzie. He jerked from her and moved to the stairs.

"Is it okay if I check out the upstairs? I need to see the breaches in security you have in this place."

"Sure."

He made his way up the curved staircase. He came to the first room on the right—her bedroom. He inhaled deeply the smell of honeysuckle, so sweet and fragrant. He looked around and found she had windows that could be accessed from the fire escape. The fire escape was probably why she chose this bedroom, but from a security standpoint, it was extremely dangerous. Her bed was adorned with a lavender comforter and matching throw pillows. He never understood throw pillows. Lizzie had them on their bed, too. Lola had two dressers, each dark mahogany to match her bed frame. She had a king sleigh bed.

His thoughts drifted to her sleeping in the bed. What he would give to wake her up with gentle kisses and nuzzle her neck, all the while inhaling her sweet fragrance, touching her soft skin. He imagined the way her body would feel under his. She was toned yet soft in the right places. He wanted to feel her ride him as he cupped her firm ass with one hand and her breast with the other. She was a remarkably beautiful woman, incredibly athletic. He was too broken for her. She deserved someone better. He shook his head and made his way back into the hallway.

The next room he encountered was the bathroom. It was spacious and luxurious like the rest of her brownstone. He found the same earth tones here as he did in the rest of the home. In fact, every room had a complementary earth tone color. All except her bedroom, painted a shade of lavender to complement her bedspread.

When he finished assessing her security or lack thereof, he returned to her in the living room. The secret of her favorite seat was now exposed as she sat on the couch's right hand side with a book in her hand. He approached so quietly, she never looked up from her book. He stood there a moment drinking in her beauty. Her long hair was draped over her shoulder, out of her way. *Was she a natural blonde?*

"You have some serious security issues with your home. For instance, anyone can enter your bedroom through the fire escape stairs and platform."

She looked up, startled by his presence. She hadn't heard him enter the room.

"You're the expert. What does that mean?" She wasn't stupid, she knew exactly what that meant, but for some reason she had to hear it come from him.

"That means my job is going to be a lot harder. Why didn't your father pay to have some high-tech security installed in your place?"

"I didn't want it. I want to live like a normal person."

"Well, until my team can neutralize the Ortiz Cartel, we will have to get a system installed—with cameras."

"Okay." She stood and walked to him. Once she was in his space, she held out her hand. "Can I borrow your cell phone please? I need to call my father to have him install his precious security system." He reached into his pocket and pulled out his phone. When he handed it to her, their fingers brushed, and the electricity that coursed between them caused both of their heads to rise and their eyes to meet. She bit her bottom lip. He groaned silently. He wanted to nibble her bottom lip, so plump, so red, so ripe.

After she asked her daddy for the system, she handed the phone to Rob.

"Yes, sir. I understand. Tonight, that would be great. Yes, sir. The sooner, the better." He pressed the end button and looked to Lola. "They will be here in a few hours to install the system. Are you hungry? I'm starving. I don't remember the last time I ate."

"Yeah, I know what you mean. I haven't eaten a solid meal in weeks. Shall we go out? I don't have anything here." She motioned to the kitchen.

"Let's hit the grocery store, and I will cook us something. Do you like broiled Mahi Mahi with arugula?

"I love Mahi Mahi. It's one of my favorites. But I can cook it. You don't have to. You're here for a different reason."

"I don't mind. I enjoy cooking."

"Why don't we cook it together?" she suggested, meeting his eyes with her hopeful ones. It was very important to show him she wasn't a spoiled princess.

Could he do this? Could he cook with another woman? A woman who wasn't his Lizzie? He looked into her eyes and saw the hope and excitement there. He couldn't let her down. "Sure. We can do that." He bowed his head and wiped at his nose. He was reliving the times he and Lizzie cooked together, too numerous to count. He rubbed the heel of his palm against his chest to rub out the pain of her memory. He tried to push the memories of Lizzie to the back of his mind, but he knew only alcohol could do that. Alcohol and now his Lola.

Again, she sensed his pain. "Do you want to talk about it?"

"No. I'm fine."

"Clearly you're not fine. What is going on? You can talk to me. I won't judge you, I promise."

"No." He turned away from her.

Not being able to stand seeing this man who she was so desperately attracted to in pain, she approached him. She stood behind him and felt the heat crackle between them like a wildfire burning out of control. She reached for his shoulder, but he shrugged her hand away. How was she going to reach him?

How was he going to forgive himself for losing Lizzie so he could finally move on? How long was he going to torture himself with her memory? When would it finally begin to fade? When would the movie and her cries stop playing in his mind?

STRONGER

Securing the outside, he led Lola to the SUV. Opening her door, he helped her inside. Once he closed her door, he rounded the vehicle and hopped in the driver's seat.

"Can you direct me to the nearest grocery store? One that will have the ingredients we need?"

"Sure. Go straight and make a right at the second light."

He pulled out onto the street with ease. Following her directions, they arrived at Whole Foods Market and he pulled into the lot and parked the car. Again, he placed his hand on her knee, and again it felt like her body had caught fire. A simple touch was too much for her.

"Stay here until I make sure we're safe. I don't think we were followed, but just let me check."

She waited patiently inside the SUV while he monitored and observed his surroundings. When nothing appeared threatening, he opened her door and extended his hand to her. Without being shy, she took his hand and this time interlocked their fingers. They held hands into the store.

They traveled down the aisle with Rob pushing the cart and Lola placing the items inside the basket. They strolled up and down every aisle. Lola took great comfort in the mundane experience of grocery shopping, especially with Rob at her side. When they turned down the spice aisle, a woman openly stared at Rob. Lola was desperately attracted to Rob and his gorgeous features, so she shouldn't be surprised other women would be too. But something about the way this woman was looking at Rob raised the hair on the back of Lola's neck. She had never felt jealousy before, but she was feeling it with a vengeance now. Lola had to stake her claim on the man by her side. She reached down and grabbed Rob's hand, interlocking their fingers together.

Rob, surprised and taken aback, jerked his head at Lola. He saw her staring at the woman who was checking him out. Wanting Lola to know he felt the same way about her, he brought her hand up and pressed his lips softly to the back of her hand.

Surprised and curious, she looked at him. His lips tugged at the corners of his mouth. Her cheeks burned at being caught acting jealous. His grin widened, and for the first time since meeting him, she saw his glorious dimples in both cheeks. That smile was worth all the embarrassment and then some. Right then she made it her mission to get him to smile like that more often, especially at her. He always looked either serious or sad. It was such a heartwarming relief to see him smile at her. It felt as if this man was going to give her a chance.

After covering all of the aisles and getting what they needed, they headed to the checkout. Rob insisted on paying. She would never understand why. It was clear she had way more money than he did. He worked for a living. She had a well-endowed trust fund. Nevertheless, she let him have his way because it brought another dimpled smile to his face.

He realized he was having a good time. It had been a long time since he felt that way. The last time he truly enjoyed himself was with Lizzie. Guilt consumed him. How dare he have a good time when Lizzie wasn't even alive anymore? He shook his head and folded back in on himself.

The real Rob was shut down once again to Lola. Rob couldn't make eye contact with her. He cast his eyes upon the ground until they stepped out of the grocery store, and then her warrior was back. Little did he know Lola was on a mission. And when she was on a mission, she could be ruthless.

Arriving back at the house, they unloaded the groceries, and Rob helped put them away. Rob got out the pan and the ingredients to cook their dinner. Lola busied herself making the marinade for the fish. Once she was finished, she handed it to Rob. Rob poured the marinade over the fish and placed it in the refrigerator for a few hours. The security installation team would be there any minute. He peeled two carrots and handed one to Lola to snack on while they waited.

The men arrived, and Rob questioned them on their level of expertise, as well as the equipment and the installation. He knew as much as they did by the time they were done.

This was no ordinary, simple system any trained criminal could bypass by turning off the power. No, this system was the best money could buy. They installed ultra-sensitive motion and body heat detectors. This was backed up with motion detectors able to tell the difference between a human and a cat on all windows and doors. Cameras were set up on the fire escape, front door, and back door, which would feed into the monitors now taking up desk space inside Lola's living room. The men had to access the roof to install the box necessary for all monitors and motion detectors. Rob would know if anyone was trying to gain entry into her brownstone. Also part of the security package was a tracker they placed on her necklace, which was chosen because they had not removed it the first time they took her, so chances were, if they got her again, they wouldn't remove it.

Her necklace meant so much to her. It had belonged to her mother. Her mother loved the ocean and so did Lola. She went every chance she got and even learned how to surf. The necklace had a seashell charm dangling from it, perfect to attach the tracker to. She didn't care, as long as they didn't break or ruin the charm. It was all she had left of her mother.

"Are they going to have to break the necklace?" she worried while she looked down at the floor. He could sense the necklace was important to her and felt an overwhelming desire to reassure her.

"No. They won't break it. Watch. They are going to place that tiny little piece inside the seashell with superglue. You can take it to a jeweler and have it removed once this is over with." He reached out his hand and ran it up and down her bare arm trying to assure her that everything was going to be okay. She had to be scared, but she sure didn't act like it. He admired that about her.

Once the tracker was installed, she was instructed to never remove the necklace, not even in the shower. Now she could be tracked from Rob's cell phone and Blackrain's office.

The men finished up, leaving Lola and Rob alone once more. Rob returned to the refrigerator and removed the fish. Lola began setting the table. Absentmindedly, she placed a candle in the center of the table and lit it. Rob had finished preparing the meal and served two plates, placing them on the placemats Lola had set out. Lola sat down after getting them drinks. She flaked off a piece of the fish and moaned at how delicious it was. "How did you learn to cook like this?" she asked, watching Rob sink back into himself. *Why did she keep losing him?* "Look, I don't know how long we are going to spend together, but I honestly would like to get to know you. What happened? You can tell me. I will understand," Lola begged Rob, wanting to ease some of his hurt.

"I lost my fiancée to a terrorist group known as the Armed Islamic Group. They operate out of Algeria, but a year and a half ago they had a cell in the states. They kidnapped her and killed her." He surprised himself. He never talked about it with anyone other than Michael or his other brothers. *What was it about her that made him so honest?*

"Rob, I am so sorry. Did she suffer?"

"I don't really want to talk about it. Let's just enjoy our meal," he said with a smile that didn't reach his sad, gray eyes.

She flaked another piece of fish and ate it with a bite of arugula. "Thank you for protecting me. Why did you decide you wanted this case?"

He couldn't tell her he wanted her like his next breath. He couldn't tell her he longed to feel her body respond to his. He couldn't tell her she cleared his mind better than any drug prescribed by the doctor could. Because doing that would be betraying Lizzie, and he couldn't do that. Lola was different than the women he slept with. Lola made everything okay. Lola eased his mind and his spirit. She made him want to be a better person. He could feel things for her. In fact, he already did.

CHAPTER SIXTEEN

After a peaceful meal enjoying each other's company, Lola got up and started to clear the table. Rob stood immediately to help her. He cleared his own place setting and brought the dish and glass into her kitchen and placed them in the dishwasher.

"I'll clean up the pots and pans. You go rest. You must be exhausted after all of this."

"No way. I'm helping. You wash, I'll dry and put away. Deal?"

He smiled a real smile at her insistence and moved aside to allow her room to work. They finished the dishes in silence.

"Do you want to have a glass of wine with me?" she asked as she peeled the covering from the top of the wine bottle.

"Here. Let me," he insisted, grabbing the corkscrew from her hand. Once she relinquished the wine bottle to his control, he opened it with minimal effort and poured two helpings of wine into the glasses she had retrieved. Her plan was to get him a little tipsy so he would open up to her. He was helping her cause by pouring an extra-large serving of the white liquid.

Glasses in hand, they retreated to the plush furniture of her living room. Before she sat, she placed her glass on the coffee table, and although it was the dead of summer, she pressed the button to ignite the gas fireplace. She was trying to create a mood. She had to get to him somehow. Her instincts, which had only been wrong once with the man who had initially kidnapped her, were not wrong now. He felt something for her. But for whatever reason, he was fighting himself. She had to get to the bottom of the mystery that was Rob. She didn't even know his last name.

He left her right hand side of the couch open and sat on the left hand side opposite her. This would never do. She had the need, the desire to be close to him, to be touching him. She picked up her glass and moved to the middle of the couch. She sat cross-legged facing his body so her knee was up against his leg. She slowly sipped her wine while she watched him gulp his. Thank God they bought several bottles at the store.

"What is your last name? Here you are risking your life for me, and I don't even know your full name," she said, smiling as seductively as possible. She looked up to meet his eyes through hooded lashes. She blinked several times. She was sending all of the right signals to this man. She might as well paint a sign on her head that read "Take me. I'm yours."

Rob took another gulp of his wine. He was drinking two glasses to her one. Getting him to open up should be easy. Rob stood and walked back into the kitchen returning with another opened bottle of wine. "My last name is Fabik," he said as he poured himself another full glass. She could tell he was uncomfortable. But surely he had to feel the sexual energy palpitating between them.

Rob had to get his urges, his craving for Lola under control. He took another large gulp of wine, hoping to dull the sensation of being near her. But the more he drank, the more he thought about touching her body in ways no man had ever touched her before. That thought alone caused a longing deep within his soul. He desperately wanted her to give herself to him.

"So. I want to talk about your fiancée," Lola said, unashamed about prying into a practical stranger's life. She sipped her wine.

"Let's not go there. It still hurts."

She was making progress. If it still hurt, that meant he still felt something for the woman. Did she still possess his heart? That was Lola's real question. Could he ever be hers?

"Which is all the more reason you need to talk about her. I'm interested. I want to know what the woman who won your heart was like." She continued under her breath, "To see if I have a chance."

Did he just hear her right? A chance? She wants a chance?

Rob felt the sting of tears at the thought of his dead fiancée. He would not break down in front of Lola. He blinked back the tears. He was a trained warrior for God's sake.

Lola reached under his chin, raised his head, and turned it so he was facing her. What he saw amazed and humbled him. She was crying. She felt for him.

Maybe he could share this pain with another person. Maybe if he did, it wouldn't be so hard to carry. He downed the last of his wine and poured himself and Lola another glass. Lola wiped at her tears with the back of her hand.

"It hurts me that you're hurting. Please let me shoulder some of your pain. I promise not to judge or even comment."

Unable to keep the truth from this woman, he confessed, "They raped her to death. They raped her while I was on the phone with her captors, and I could hear her in the background. I could hear her cries, her grunts, her moans as she begged them to stop. But they didn't. They raped her so badly and so many times, they caused internal hemorrhaging and she bled to death." He exhaled, feeling lighter than he had felt in years. Lola reached for him, but he pulled away.

"Don't you get it? I couldn't save her. The one person above all others who I should have been able to protect, to save, and I failed. I'm broke. I'm no good to anyone." The despair he felt was rising up again, threatening to consume him. He knew he needed to forgive himself, but he didn't know how.

"Have you tried talking to her?" Lola asked as she gently caressed his shoulder and then his arms. She ran her fingers lightly over his taut skin, tickling him with her long nails.

"What do you mean?" he asked.

"Have you been to her gravesite and really talked to her? Told her how you feel?"

What was it about the simplicity of her suggestion that made so much sense to him? "Who did you lose?" he inquired knowing she knew the pain of losing someone.

"My mother. It wasn't as awful as losing your fiancée. She overdosed, so it was her own fault, her choice, but I felt the pain all the same."

"Don't do that. Don't discount your loss just because your mother could have prevented her death."

"That's just it. My mother, were she a stronger person, could have prevented her death. Your fiancée couldn't have. And although we both lost someone, I am sure your loss is much harder on you because of the way it happened."

"This isn't a contest. We both lost someone we loved and cared for. Did you visit your mom's gravesite to talk to her? Did it help?"

"When it first happened, I couldn't even think about talking to her; I was so mad at her for what she had done. But after a while, I realized the only person being harmed by my anger was me. So, I went to her one day and laid it all out there. I told her exactly how I felt about her and why I was so angry. I told her how I would only forgive her for myself, but would never forget what she did to me by overdosing. And it did help. I got it all off my chest, and I told it to the one person who could take the pain away."

"You do that, you know."

"Do what?"

"Make the pain go away. When I'm around you, I don't think about her as much."

Lola's cheeks blushed. She never, in her wildest fantasies—and she had some wild ones—imagined a tough, warrior, her protector, confessing his feelings so freely to her. She rationalized he must want her to know.

"You still need to talk to her. Say we can go tomorrow. Say you will talk to her and tell her everything you just told me. She needs to hear it, and you need to say it to her."

He had hidden behind the pain for the last year and a half. What would it be like to lessen that pain? What if talking to Lizzie gave him the strength to forgive himself? Could he start something with Lola? Would she want him? He knew he had to put Lizzie behind him to have any chance with Lola.

"Will you come with me? I don't want to go alone. And I can't leave you by yourself," he said behind a cough trying to minimize his vulnerability around her. He was a warrior for Christ's sake. He had killed men. He had saved men. Yet he couldn't save his Lizzie. Would talking to her really ease his pain? He looked up through his dark lashes and caught the cool blue pools of someone who understood. She wasn't trying to fix him; she was just trying to give him some closure. He felt himself being drawn to her. He couldn't stop his approach as he came within a hairsbreadth of Lola's lips. The gentlest of touches, the barest of whispers, her soft lips pressed gently to his. His head began to swim with desire. He felt Lola's being to the depth of his soul. He knew with her by his side he could do anything, even forgive himself and move on. Because he wanted so desperately to move on with Lola.

Lola felt his firm lips start to gentle against hers. She felt tingles spread into her stomach and pull between her legs. Just one kiss and she felt her panties dampen. She had heard about it but had never experienced it. His lips melted to hers as he turned his head slightly, using his tongue to lick her bottom lip. The heat inside her turned up a notch, as if that were even possible. She slowly parted her lips to allow his tongue access to her mouth. He took his time, gently exploring her lips and mouth with his tongue. She closed her lips around his tongue and mimicked a slight suckling. He groaned into her mouth and moved his hand into the back of her hair, bringing her mouth closer to his. She released his tongue and met it with her own. Their tongues touched and tangled in each other's mouth. She felt the pressure on the back of her head pulling her closer and became dripping wet. No one had ever affected her this way. She wanted him with everything she was and all that she could ever be.

He loosened his hold on the back of her head and wrapped her long hair around his hand. He lightly pulled her head back, breaking their connection. He knew she was a virgin. He also knew she would give her greatest gift to him, if he only asked. But he couldn't ask, not until he was ready to give himself to her fully. She met his eyes and smiled a bright white grin at him. He returned in kind, showing her the dimples she loved so much. Tonight was going to be a long night indeed.

STRONGER

"Tomorrow," he promised.

CHAPTER
SEVENTEEN

The sleeping arrangements were hard for Lola to handle. She wanted nothing more than to be wrapped in Rob's strong, muscular arms after their earth shattering kiss. Rob walked her upstairs and double checked the alarm sensors on her windows. Once he was sure she would be protected, he walked down her hallway to the spare bedroom. Lola stood at the door making sure he had everything he needed.

"I'm going to grab a shower before turning in. Do you need anything else?" Lola asked in a soft, charming voice.

"Nope. I'm all set."

Lola padded down the hallway to her bathroom. It wasn't a spacious room, but it did have enough room for a shower and a separate tub. She opted for a bath after the ordeals she had been through. She got out the lavender liquid and poured some into the water. She lit a few candles and turned off the lights. A nice, relaxing bubble bath was exactly what she needed.

She cupped her hands in the water and poured it over her breasts, making her nipples hard. She blew on them as she liked to watch them peak. She liked to watch the water run down her body to be rejoined with the bathwater. She played with the bubbles, pushing them up over her breasts, making a makeshift bra for her to wear while in the bath. While playing with the bubbles, her hand brushed against one of her erect nipples and her mind instantly thought it was Rob's hand. She rolled her nipple between her thumb and forefinger, slightly pinching it. Imagining Rob, she slid her hand under the bubbles, into the water, to touch her swollen nub. She applied pressure while she moved her fingers in a circular motion over and around her clit. Her back arched as she slid one finger inside of herself. She pictured Rob's hands on her body as she moved her hand in and out of her body. She used two fingers now, bringing herself nearer to climax. She pictured Rob's body, naked and standing in front of her. In her mind she could see his ripped abs and muscular arms. She increased her speed, taking care to hit her clit with her palm each time she slid her fingers inside. She imagined his stormy gray eyes delighting in the sight of her touching herself. She was warm and wet and her two fingers stretched her out. She took herself back to the kiss. She felt the way his lips pressed against hers. The memory sparked her assent into bliss. She moaned his name out loud as she came hard around her fingers.

When she came back into herself, she washed her body and her hair. She stepped out of the tub and towel dried her hair. Finally, she wrapped the towel firmly around her body, tucking it tightly against her before she opened the door. To her surprise, Rob was waiting outside. *Had he heard her call his name?* If he did he wasn't trying to save her the embarrassment as both dimples were showing as he smiled at her.

"Have a nice shower?" he asked, smiling like the cat that just ate the canary.

"Yes, thank you," she replied, breathing more heavily than she wanted to. She felt her cheeks flame at his knowing smile. She moved past him to her bedroom, but he reached out and grabbed her arm. He pushed her roughly into the wall next to the bathroom door. He brought his arms up and placed each one next to her head, caging in her body in with his. Slowly, methodically, like a hunter stalks his prey, he stepped into her until she felt his tight body pressed firmly against hers. With torturous slowness, he moved in for their second kiss. He crept closer to her mouth, drawing out the anticipation. Once he reached her, he placed his hot mouth over her parted lips. He devoured her in a soul-altering kiss. He wrapped her wet hair firmly around his hand and roughly angled her head to accept his demands. She could feel his erection pressed against her lower abdomen.

He broke the kiss and growled, "I heard you say my name." He didn't say it to embarrass her. He just wanted her to know he was thinking about her as much as she was thinking about him.

"You did?" she whispered, ashamed, and she looked down to where their bodies joined.

"I did," he said, "and I liked how it sounded coming from your mouth." He smiled that dazzling, panty-dropping smile complete with double dimples.

She raised her eyes to meet his. In his eyes all the desire and passion was reflected back to her. Tentatively, she moved in to kiss him this time. She was soft and gentle. She brushed her lips over his and it was he that moaned. Mimicking him from earlier, she licked his bottom lip and then sucked it into her mouth and gently nipped at it. She was rewarded with his hard body pressing firmly into hers. Her breasts molded to his hard chest. He ran his hand up her thigh. He stopped just short of her center, making lazy circles with his fingers. He trailed his trim, cut nails down her leg and back up, each time sending sparks through her body. She curled her toes and deepened the kiss. She gave him back control as he sucked both of her lips into his mouth. She ran her hands down his sides to the hem of his shirt. She wanted to feel his skin pressed against hers. As she tugged at the hem, he stepped away from her, breaking the connection. He lifted the shirt over his head. She took in all that he was: his beautiful, well-defined upper body, each sinew like chiseled marble.

He stalked closer to her and reached for her towel. He wanted her naked and under him. She was all he could think of at that moment.

She hesitated. No man had ever seen her naked. No man other than the ones who had kidnapped her. She shook her head. She wanted this, wanted this man who stood gloriously in front of her, pressed against her. Yet she wrapped both arms firmly around the towel at her chest. *She wanted him, that was for certain, but was she ready for this*? She knew he had to have control. It came through in the way he kissed her, in the way he controlled her body with his. He was playing her body to a song only he could hear. He met her defiant gaze. Her chin protruding outward like she was going to fight him. He smiled and she was lost to him.

Slowly, her arms came down to her sides. He reached for the towel and removed the tightly tucked corner. Before it could drop, he held it and dropped it onto the floor next to his feet. He took a step back to admire the perfection that was her body. Although she didn't have a six-pack, the skin across her stomach was stretched taut. The definition in her arms showed even as they hung at the side of her body. And her breasts. They were perfect, a little more than a handful, and he had big hands. They were perky and ripe. He had never gazed at anyone or anything so beautiful in his life.

"You're fucking beautiful," he said with reverence in his voice.

She knew she was pretty, but the way he said it made her believe it for the first time in forever. She never felt more beautiful than she did with Rob caressing her with his eyes.

He lingered on her breasts before moving his eyes down to the apex between her legs. He loved the gap between her legs. Perfect for his hand to fit and she wouldn't have to move. And her legs were as equally toned as her arms. She was perfection. He moved quickly, pressing his chest against her ample bosom. He felt the jolt, an electric current pass down over his spine. He felt it again in his groin as his sac pulled against his cock. He was painfully erect. To make Lola aware of exactly what she could do to him, he pressed his erection into her lower abdomen.

She moaned at the feel of his shirtless body against hers. She knew, in that moment, he was the one. He was the one she would give herself to. He was worthy of her gift. She started to move her hips, trying to create friction with his body. She wanted him to want her like she wanted him—with his entire being, body and soul.

"Patience, Lola. Anticipation is one of the best parts." He kissed her fiercely with all of his pent-up desire he had been feeling since first laying eyes on her in that white negligee. He reached around and grabbed her ass, pulling her body closer to him. She wrapped a leg around his body, resting her foot on his ass, and pulled him into her. With his right hand he traced the leg that was wrapped around him from knee to thigh to her center. In contrast to how he was kissing her, he gently touched the core of her being. He could feel her slickness, her desire running down her thigh. She was so responsive to him.

He growled. "I will never let anything happen you to. You have to believe me. I know what I told you, but please, believe me. I will die before anyone harms you," he swore to her in a low, breathy voice.

"I know," was all she said.

It was enough. He slid one finger inside her and marveled at how tight she was. He imagined what it would be like to take her for the first time as he removed his finger and ran it up and down over her clit. She was still sensitive from her orgasm in the bathtub, so she tried to stop him. She pushed against his hand to move it away. He wouldn't allow it. From now on, he would be the one bringing her pleasure. He would see to it that she was taken care of in all ways. She didn't know it yet, but she was his. He slid his finger back into her as she arched her back, pressing her breasts into his chest. Each time he would remove his finger and run it up and down the length of her clit, she moved closer to climax.

"I want to watch you this time. I've heard you. Now I want to watch you when you come. I want to watch the way your lips form my name. Only *my* name as *my* body brings you the pleasure you deserve," he whispered with hot breath into her ear, causing goose bumps to spring up all over her body. This was the farthest she had ever gone with a man, but with Rob, it felt right. Everything about him felt right to her. He dipped his finger back into her and she moaned. She was so close. Sliding his finger back into her, he was sure to hit her clit with his thumb. He moved in and out at a tireless rhythm, causing her to break and fall over the edge.

"Rob," she moaned as her body fell out into the universe; the universe showing her the heavens behind her tightly closed eyes. She saw specks of light as her orgasm overtook her. Her legs felt weak, but his strong arms were wrapped so tightly around her body, she knew she was safe. This wasn't her first orgasm. She masturbated all the time, but this was her most intense.

She could only dream of what sex would be like with him.

"Mine," he growled into her ear, causing a fire to burn deep within her body. She agreed; she was his, but that was her secret to keep.

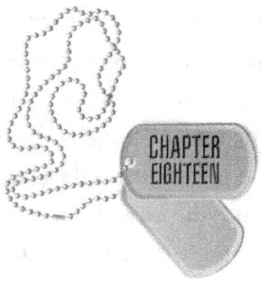

Rob bent over and picked up the towel strewn on the floor. He handed it back to Lola. Feeling embarrassed, she wrapped the towel tightly around her body, covering everything Rob had just worshipped.

"I guess we better get some sleep," Rob said, sensing her embarrassment. He had to know. "Have you ever done that before? What we just did?"

"No," she whispered as her face flamed red, and she felt the burn upon her cheeks.

"Did you enjoy it?" Rob asked in a breathy voice. He was breathing hard at the knowledge that he was her first. He heard his heart pounding in his ears as he awaited her response. What if he took it too far and pushed her away. What would he do then? He had to have her; he had to make her his—his to possess, his to own, his to pleasure. He noticed the pulse jump in her neck. No matter what she said, he knew she enjoyed it.

She would never lie to him. His eyes demanded the truth. She wanted a relationship with this man who she hardly knew, this man who had saved her life.

"It was amazing," she said, unable to make eye contact. She wasn't a shy woman, but things felt different with Rob; she didn't want to scare him away.

Before, with men, she was brazen and bold because she knew nothing was ever going to happen between the man she was dancing with, or on a date with, and her. But now it was the exact opposite. She knew she would willingly give herself to him—the greatest gift she could give the man who saved her life. A man who spent his own money to rescue her. Just because she didn't care about money didn't mean he felt the same. And $25,000 was a lot to spend on a woman he didn't know. Why had he spent his own money?

She started to move past Rob to go to her bedroom to get dressed. He was still so close to her that she could smell his unique scent. He smelled divine. She lingered a moment as if she was going to say something, then shook her head and continued to walk to her bedroom. Rob followed. She reached into her dresser and pulled out her night clothes. Normally, she slept in panties and nothing else, but with Rob in the house, she felt compelled to dress.

"Why did you do it? Why did you spend your own money to save me?" She had to know if it was just the mission or something more.

"I wanted to own you," he said, stalking closer to her. He closed the distance in three long strides.

"Own me? What do you mean? No man owns me. My father still thinks he does, and you saw how I feel about that."

"I want to own you, Lola. I have from the moment I first laid eyes on you in the barn. Something about you touched a part of me that has been closed for a long time. Something about you made me feel. I don't want to go back to how I was. I want to own you, to know you will never leave, to know I am the only one who gets to bring you pleasure like I did in the hallway, to know I have the privilege of taking care of you and providing for you, to know you are mine."

"Wow."

"I don't mean to scare you away. I know it's a lot to take in."

"I want all of those things," she whispered. *Could she have those things with Rob?* "All my life I have been groomed to be someone I'm not. I've had to be seen with the right people, attend the right parties, shop at the right stores—all dictated by my father. I want my own life. I want a family, a large family, full of love and laughter. The kind I never had." She bowed her head and squeezed her eyes shut, trying to fight back the tears. He lifted her chin to look into those glassy blue eyes. He wiped his thumb across her check. He bent forward and gently pressed his lips to her cheek, kissing each tear away.

How could he tell her kids weren't in the cards for him? His life was too dangerous. He wouldn't want to bring kids into the world to be used against him on a mission. He would put a gun to his head then. He would still have her; he just had to figure out a way around the kid issue.

"I don't want to control your life, Lola. I want to own you. So I know you will always be mine. There is a big difference."

"This is crazy. We just met each other. We don't even know each other."

"I beg to differ. I know what you want. I know about your secrets, and more importantly, you know about mine. I would say right now, no one knows me better."

"What about all of the things only time teaches?"

"I'm willing to learn if you are. Who was it that said we had to follow a timeframe or a pattern when it comes to being together? We are two consenting adults. When we feel the time is right, then the time is right. I will not play games with you, Lola."

"I won't play games with you either."

"So, you want to do this. I did already pay for you," he bantered with a quirk to his lip, trying to lighten the mood.

"Which reminds me. Why did you spend your own money for me? Are you rich? Is that amount of money nothing to you?"

"Are you kidding?! That was half of my savings. I just couldn't let someone else claim you. I had to win you."

"Win me, huh? And how do you plan on doing that?" she asked as she rose up on her toes and brought her soft lips to meet his.

"Like this," he said before taking her and demanding she open her mouth to him. He thrust his tongue inside, exploring her. He licked her lips and sought out her tongue. Their tongues touched, causing a fire to burn deep within both of their bellies. A fire and an emptiness that only the other could fill. He firmed his tongue and continued his exploration. Being the tease that she was, she closed her lips around his tongue and suckled it, drawing it deeper into her mouth. She mimicked suckling his cock. He moaned a deep tone from his throat. He could only imagine her lips wrapped around his cock, sucking and licking. He placed his hands on her shoulders and pushed her away from him in one move, shaking his head.

"We better stop, or I'm not going to be able to."

She stood there, surprised. She wanted him and was trying to make it painfully obvious. *Did he just reject her?* She felt rejected, bereft.

"Sorry," she said, looking out of the window, anywhere but his eyes.

"Don't you dare do that! Don't you dare think I don't want you, Lola. You have to know; you have to feel it." He lifted her hand and placed it brazenly against his cock. "That is what you do to me. I. Want. You. Desperately. But, I also know you are a virgin, and so I am willing to wait until you're ready."

A gentleman. She wouldn't have thought it. She would have thought he would be trying everything he could to get into her panties, to claim her.

"I think you just won me," she mumbled, more to herself than to Rob. But Rob heard and his lips tugged up at the corners, causing one dimple to appear. She didn't see his triumph. She was still looking out of the window trying to calm herself. She was so turned on— she wanted him so badly. She was ready. *Maybe he wasn't.*

"I should let you get dressed and get some sleep. It's been a long day."

"It's been a long two weeks," she responded as she moved to her bedroom door. She stood, hand propped against the edge of the door, waiting for him to leave her room. He got the hint and followed her to the door.

"I will let you get dressed and get to bed. I'm right down the hall if you need anything. If you sense something isn't right, come and get me. Use every instinct you have to protect yourself. If you wake up with an uneasy feeling, that something isn't right, come to get me or just yell my name."

"Okay," she said closing the door behind him. Once the door was closed, she leaned her back against it for support. She had come so close to giving herself to him tonight. But maybe he wasn't ready. After everything he had been through, Lola knew he probably needed to speak with Lizzie first before they could be together. She would wait for him. He was worth it.

On the other side of the door, Rob rested with his back against it. He had forgotten completely about his Lizzie. And damn if he didn't feel guilty. This time, not for forgetting about her, but because he enjoyed being free of her ghost and feeling again. And damn did he feel for Lola. He felt more for Lola than he ever dreamt he could or would feel for another human being. Losing her was not an option. He didn't like the idea of sleeping down the hall in a spare room. But he knew she needed her space. The last thing he wanted to do was to come on too strong and scare her away.

He made up his mind. He would talk to Lizzie the way Lola had suggested. They would go tomorrow. He would have the company jet brought down, and he would fly Lola to meet his Lizzie. He had to stop thinking about Lizzie as his. *She was dead.* And for the first time in a year and a half, he admitted it. It took Lola, but he could finally admit Lizzie was dead.

STRONGER

Rob laid there in his soft, comfortable queen-size bed in Lola's guest room. His comforter had tiny wild flowers on it, as did the curtains in the room. This room was definitely meant for a woman. No matter, he was comfortable. He just couldn't fall asleep. He would let nothing happen to Lola. Nothing. He listened for every noise, every creak, every moan the brownstone made. He listened and tried to learn the noises of the house. It was imperative he learned what was normal so he could distinguish danger. He laid there staring at the ceiling, the moonlight peeking through the sheer panels which covered the windows. The heavy curtains were tied back with a matching piece of fabric. He should get up and close them.

He sat up and heard something strange. He heard feet padding down the hallway, like someone was trying to be as quiet as possible. He grabbed his gun from the nightstand table and went to the door. He stood behind it, readying himself to throw it open and be confronted by the men who were here to gather his Lola. He smiled. His Lola. It had a nice ring to it. He shook his head. Just then the door handle started to turn. He took a step back from his hidden position behind the door. He would let the bastards come into the room and then take them out.

Lola quietly peeked into the room. When she didn't see Rob in the bed, she stepped fully inside.

Rob pulled his gun, unsure who was on the other side. He reached for the doorknob, and with one quick movement, pulled the door all the way open. He drew his gun and pointed it directly at Lola. She screamed.

"Shit. I'm so sorry. I thought you were the bad guys."

She had her hand over her heart and felt it beat in the back of her throat. He really scared her. She stood there trembling. He pulled her into his arms and wrapped his muscular arms around her tight body. She wasn't little. She stood at a cool five foot ten without heels. He was only slightly taller than her at six foot three. Still, her cheek rested nicely against his neck. He held her in his embrace until she stopped shaking. When she was ready and not a minute before, she broke the embrace.

"Care to tell me what you were doing peeking into my room," he bantered, showing both dimples.

"I couldn't sleep."

"Me either. I am too worried about you to sleep."

She was still in his space, and he could smell her wonderful honeysuckle fragrance. *Is it a body lotion she uses to smell that good?* How he longed to lose himself inside her. Lose himself to her smell. Lose himself to her.

"Do you feel like something isn't right? Are you listening to your instincts about what's going on around you?" he asked, because he would check the entire goddamned neighborhood if that's what it took to make her feel safe.

"I am listening to my instincts, yes," she said as she moved closer to him. "I am listening because they are screaming at me. They are telling me to do this," she said before closing her soft, full lips over his surprised opened ones. She sought out his tongue with hers. They danced and then she suckled his bottom lip into her mouth and bit down on it. He went instantly hard.

This time he wasn't going to be the gentleman. She had sought him out. She came to him. She was ready. She just told him so with her achingly beautiful kiss.

"I want that too, love," he said, bringing his finger up to touch the lip she made bleed. "But your first time has to be tender, gentle. I won't have it any other way. Are you sure you want it to be with me?"

"We are both consenting adults," she threw his words back at him. "We say when the time is right. I have been lying in bed for the last two hours thinking of your touch, of your kiss, of your sexy hands."

"You think these are sexy?" he asked holding them up in front of him for her to get a better look in the moonlit room. They were large and tanned. The veins in his hands protruded against his skin.

"Yes. I think they are incredibly sexy. Especially when they are touching my soft body." She was making it very hard for him to say no. She pressed herself flush against him. Her large breasts molded to his hard chest. He could feel her erect nipples against his bare chest. She had caught him in nothing but his boxer briefs. And what was she wearing?

She came to seduce him. She had on a sexy lace negligee. The body of the piece was red and see-through. He could just make out her darkened areolas. He had to taste her. He ran his calloused finger down her arm and her hand. Once he reached the underside of her hand, he intertwined their fingers together.

"I want you to know what you are getting yourself into, love," he cautioned. "I have done some pretty bad things. I have done these bad things for good reasons. Some would call me a murderer, some, a torturer, and they wouldn't be wrong. I have murdered men; I have tortured men. I have had missions where I have killed so many men in one hour it's impossible for me to know how many. I have done all of this without batting an eye, without guilt. I served five tours in war-torn Afghanistan. I have killed women and children who meant to do me harm; they haunt me every night. You could do much better than me. For God's sake, I'm still in love with my dead fiancée. But, if after knowing all of this, you still say you want me, I won't stop this thing between us. Not again. Know that!"

"Do you want to know what I see? I see a man who is tortured by the things he has done. I see you. I see your pain and your guilt. I see it in the smile that doesn't reach your eyes. I see it in the way you are still in love with a woman you couldn't save. I see the man that you are: tough and humble. God, look at you. You're gorgeous. You could have any woman you want, but you say you want to own me. Who does that? Who wants to possess someone so completely their every need is cared for? You are honest and you have integrity. You aren't afraid of a challenge. The way you stood up to my dad for me. *The way you stood up for me.* No one has ever had the balls to go against my father, the rich and powerful Mr. Sardeson. The way you saved me from a life unimaginable. I want this. I want this because you're the first man I have met whom I deem worthy. You are worthy of the only gift I can give to you. You don't value money the way everyone my whole life has. Hell, you spent half your savings on a woman you didn't even know. I want to give myself to you. I want to know what it feels like to be yours."

He swallowed the lump in his throat. She had touched his soul with her words. She had touched him. She saw him and still wanted him. He tugged her hand to pull her closer to the bed. But she stayed rooted to the spot. He raised his eyebrows quizzically to her. She pulled back. "I want you in my bed."

He allowed her to pull him to her bedroom. They walked inside and stood before the bed. He reached for the hem of her negligee. She lifted her arms over her head, and he removed the sexy piece of clothing. She stood before him in a pair of red, lacy panties and a smile. Her long hair covered each breast. He stepped closer to her, resting his hands over the strings of her thong as he dipped his head and kissed her neck. He placed gentle kisses down her neck to her collarbone.

He licked along her collarbone down to her breasts. He stood back, admiring the sight before him.

"You are fucking perfect. There aren't words to describe your beauty."

He reached for her hand and placed it on her breast, covering her hand with his. He made her hand palm her breast. Before he knew it, she was palming her own breast, and he was feeling her do it. With his hand still covering hers, he ran their hands down her stomach to the top of her red, lacy panties. Using his hand to guide hers under her panties, he pushed her index finger inside her pussy. He wanted to taste her. He used his hand to push her finger in and out of her center. Slowly, he brought her index finger to his lips. "I want to taste you," he said, meeting both of her eyes. He could feel his heart pounding in his chest. He suckled her finger into his mouth, tasting her, never breaking eye contact. Slowly, he pulled her finger out of his mouth, sucking on it as he did. A wicked grin curved his lips as he removed her finger and let go of her hand.

She could feel her wetness drip down her inner thigh. She was so wanton with him, so aroused.

He could smell her arousal, her sex, and it beckoned to him like nothing ever had. He kissed her passionately as he backed her into the mattress.

He hooked his thumbs in the sides of her panties and pulled them down her gorgeous legs. She lifted her feet until she was free of them. He pushed down on her shoulder, indicating for her to sit. She sat on the bed, naked and wanting. He pushed her back so she was lying on the bed and he kneeled. He shouldered his way between her legs and saw the holy chalice; she was neatly trimmed. He used his big fingers to spread the folds of her sex. Noticing her arousal was dripping down her thigh, he bent forward and licked at it, lapping it up with his tongue. He continued to clean her of her arousal on both sides of her thighs before bringing his hot mouth to her swollen nub. He fluttered over her clit. She curved her back, bringing her center closer to his face. With that movement, he started lapping at her clit from its base to its top. He circled it with his tongue and flicked over it in pressurized strokes. He had brought her close, but he had to make sure she came because with her, the first time, he wasn't going to last very long. He slid his big finger inside her pussy.

"Holy shit, you're tight."

He continued to use his finger, moving it in and out of her center as he suckled on her clit while flicking it with his tongue. The combination drove her wild. She started bucking her hips into his face trying to get the perfect angle. He went back to tirelessly flicking her clit while thrusting his finger deeper and deeper into her. He was the whole way up to his knuckle. And yet she still bucked. She reached down and grabbed a handful of his hair, directing his head up and down her clit.

"Oh my God, Rob. I'm coming!" she screamed into the room. Her scream echoed off the walls and got caught in his head. He loved to hear the pleasure he gave her. For him, once a day wouldn't be enough.

He removed his finger and sucked it clean while his stormy gray eyes connected with hers. The move was so erotic, it lit a different type of fire within her. She wanted him inside her. She wanted to break for this man. She wanted him to own her.

"Do you promise?" she asked, almost afraid she would ruin the mood.

"What would you like me to promise?"

"That you will own me?"

"I promise, Lola. You are mine. I own you now. No one, and I mean no one, will ever have you. You belong to me."

"I have no experience, so you'll have to teach me."

"Love, I have a feeling you know more than you think you do. Just let go. Let your body take over. Do what feels good. Do only what feels natural. Everything. Everything is for your pleasure."

"Please, Rob. I need you. I need you inside of me."

Rob kissed her swollen clit and continued kissing and nipping at her skin in a straight line up the center of her body. When he reached her breasts, he paid them homage. Then he continued his way onto the bed, bracing himself with his forearms.

"I don't think you are going to fit," Lola said, scared for the first time that night.

"I will go slowly, but it is going to hurt at first. Are you ready?"

She nodded while keeping eye contact with Rob. She lost herself in the storm that was his eyes. He broke contact and reached down into his pants pocket for his wallet. He reached in and pulled out a foil packet. She didn't even have to ask as he sheathed himself with the condom.

He positioned himself at her entrance and she tensed. He rubbed the head of his cock over her wet lips before he pushed his head in and melted at how tight she was. "Holy fuck," he moaned. He pushed himself slowly into her. He wasn't the entire way inside but enough that he knew he broke her hymen. She moaned, but this moan was one of pain.

"It will get better now. I'm going to stay still until you adjust to me being inside you," he cajoled while he held her eyes. Before long it was Lola who was moving. She made little thrusts with her hips to encourage him to move. So he did. He started moving slowly out of her. As he did, her legs went around his body and she dug her heels into his ass. She pressed into him causing him to press into her. With one thrust, his balls were against her ass. He withdrew and thrust again. She wanted rhythm. That's what her hips were saying. Withdrawing, he thrust against Lola's hips. She was meeting him thrust for thrust. Their dance started to increase in tempo. He moved faster inside her, but as he did so, he brought himself closer to climax. He had never experienced anything like the feel of Lola. She was so tight and so untouched, he was honored by her gift. A gift he would forever cherish. He couldn't hold on much longer as he thrust and withdrew, thrust and withdrew.

"Harder," Lola begged. Rob thrust with such force he knocked her headboard into her wall over and over again. Her body was sliding up near the headboard with each thrust.

"Rob, I'm going to come. I'm going to come on your cock. Would you like that?" she cooed into his ear. He pressed his lips to hers and kissed her with a passion he had never known. She screamed into his mouth as she melted into the man who was there to catch her. He followed right behind her. His body went rigid as he released his seed inside the only woman who could so effectively own him.

When he came down from his orgasmic high, he got off of her, already feeling the loss of her touch. He rolled onto his side and she onto hers. They faced each other, staring into each other's eyes. He wanted to feel her pressed against his body. "Roll over so I can spoon you," he dictated. She complied and rolled onto her opposite side. His hand went around her body and rested on her stomach. He splayed his fingers and realized he was covering most of her stomach with his one hand. God, she was perfect. *Now, how did he keep her?*

Ortiz's men had watched as the contractors installed a security system in her home. They had also watched as the same men made their way to the roof to connect the box to the monitors. There was a reason Ortiz hired them for this job. His instructions were to bring the woman back to Mexico, unharmed. And that is exactly what they were going to do. They waited until a Brownstone in the vicinity of Lola's was unoccupied for the evening before rounding the back and breaking in through the back door. They found the window that contained access to the fire escape. Opening the window, each man made his way onto the landing and began climbing the ladder that led to the roof. Once there, it was as simple as walking onto Lola's roof.

There they found the box that was locked with a padlock. The taller man reached into his bag and removed a cordless drill and a drill bits box. He chose the appropriate bit and starting drilling at the keyhole. Once he drilled out the keyhole, it was a simple matter of forcing the locking mechanism up. He placed a flathead screw driver into the hole and turned it in the same direction he would have turned the key. Once he had the box open, he cut the wire for the motion detectors. They would have the woman back to Mexico in no time, and they would collect their fee from Ortiz.

Padlocks were only there to keep out the honest thieves. God knew, he wasn't honest.

STRONGER

Lola opened her eyes and was staring at a beautiful sleeping man. The sun hadn't started its ascent into the sky as the room was still dark, darker than the night with no moonlight. She reached closer to Rob and placed a gentle kiss against his closed mouth. His lips felt so soft. She didn't want to wake him. She was going to bring him breakfast in bed. She wanted Rob to know she knew how to take care of a man like him. She wanted to show him how she felt about him. Quietly, she padded her way to her dresser and pulled on a pair of denim shorts with a pink tank top. It would probably be another hot day in the middle of a Boston summer. She padded out of the room, down the hallway, down the steps, and into her kitchen. She reached for the frying pan from under her counter. She found the perfect pan for flipping pancakes and set it on the counter. She hummed to herself, feeling lighter and freer than she had ever felt before.

She gave herself to Rob last night and it was perfect. He was perfect. She wouldn't let him walk out of her life without a fight. Now that she tasted what being his felt like, she wanted nothing more. She wanted to become his. She needed to be his. She reached high into the cabinet to grab the pancake mix. The song she hummed was "All of Me" by John Legend. She really did feel Rob had all of her. Unfortunately, she didn't have all of him yet. She had to help him forgive himself because that's just want she wanted: all of him. She didn't want his guilt weighing on him like it did now. She knew he felt personally responsible for the loss of Lizzie. If he didn't, she wouldn't be able to see it in his pained stare, his clenching jaw. Who dictates how long it takes a person to truly know another? There are people who are together their whole lives and never truly know each other. Who was to say they didn't really know each other already?

Knowing him was what led her to give herself to him. He was wounded but strong. He was brave yet frightened of losing his heart again. That's the reason he had to possess her so completely. That's the reason he needed for her to agree to be possessed by him. She wouldn't do it. Not until his smile was no longer broken. He was on his way. She had a few glimpses of his real smile, the one that showed his dimples. The one that took her breath away. The one that had her craving to do things like lick those dimples. If she had it her way, he would constantly be smiling that dimple-showing, panty-dropping smile. She started towards the refrigerator by the back door. While she was retrieving the eggs, she felt someone grab hold of her arm. She was about to turn around and yell at Rob for ruining the surprise when she felt the wet rag cover her nose and mouth. She gasped and inhaled the sweet gas smell of chloroform. The eggs went crashing to the floor as Lola lost consciousness.

Rob opened his eyes to the light that filtered into the room. He never slept this good, not since before his time in the Army. He definitely didn't sleep that well after losing his Lizzie. Thoughts of Lizzie started to take hold in his mind until he remembered where he was. He looked to his left to make sure he wasn't dreaming. He was really with Lola last night. What he saw caused him to bolt up straight in bed. Lola wasn't there. He looked around. He was in Lola's room—the lilac purple walls, the darker purple comforter with matching curtains. The pillows he had thrown last night still on the floor. But no Lola. He got up and hurried to pull up his pants. He grabbed his gun from the side table and moved quietly into the hallway. He checked the bathroom: empty. He cleared the other rooms just in case. No Lola. He crept down the hallway to the stairs. He stayed silent a moment, listening for sounds. Nothing.

He made his way down the stairs as silently as possible. He didn't want to scare her, but at the same time, he didn't want to take any chances. Empty. "Lola!" he yelled. There was no response. He rushed to the front door; the deadbolt and chain lock were still in place. He moved quickly to the back door. "Fuck," he cried when he noticed the deadbolt was open. Surely she wouldn't leave without telling him. He turned around, looked into the kitchen, and froze. His wide eyes stared at the dozen eggs shattered and oozing across the kitchen floor. Panic filled his body. He started to tremble as his fists clenched at his side. He crushed his teeth together, grinding them against each other. His veins popped up through his skin. They covered his arms and hands. He reached up to rub his brow and felt the vein bulging on his forehead. He wasn't sure what that sound was and then he realized that is was his guttural roar.

He rushed to the monitors sitting atop her desk in the living room. *How could he have not heard anything? How did they get past the security system? How could he let this happen? Again?* Lizzie. Lola. He had failed them both! He felt the lump rise in the back of his throat as he rewound the disc that recorded last night's events. He pushed forward until he saw Lola enter the kitchen. She had no clue there was a man behind her. He watched helpless as the man lowered Lola's unconscious body to the ground. He checked the time stamp: 0545 hours. He looked at the clock on the wall: 0757 hours. How did he sleep through it? He should have sensed something wasn't right. He was a trained Green Beret after all.

"Fuck!" he cried as he crumbled to the ground. He couldn't lose her, not now, not when he was starting to get his life back; not when he had such deep feelings for her. Not after last night, the most amazing night of his life. He had to find her.

He straightened from his crumpled position on the floor and stood with a new purpose. He wouldn't fail this time. This time he would get the girl. He would save Lola. He had to; he didn't have a choice. He would get Lola back or die trying. The warrior was back. Feelings he hadn't felt since Afghanistan resurfaced. He didn't fear death; he feared Lola's death while he was still alive. He lifted his hand to his corded neck and began to rub while he paced back and forth, devising a plan. He would need his team. He would find out where Ortiz's Cartel was located and take down every one of those motherfuckers. No one messed with what was his. For all intents and purposes, that was Lola. She may not have agreed to it yet, but after last night, she was his. He needed to save her to save himself. He picked up his phone from the coffee table and keyed in Tony's number.

STRONGER

CHAPTER
TWENTY-ONE

Rob paced as he waited for Tony to answer his phone. He finally heard Tony's voice on the third ring. "Hello."

Rob's voice cracked. "They have her."

"Wait, what? Who has who? Someone has Lola?" Tony asked.

"They took her two hours ago. I need to come in. Now. I need the jet."

"I will fly it to you myself," Tony reassured his friend. "Other than her being gone, what happened? Something's going on with you. I can hear it in your voice. It cracked my friend. What's going on?"

"I can't lose her. I was just getting to a place that I liked. Do you know I slept in this morning? That's how she was taken. I was fucking sleeping. Tell me, Tony, you know me, when was the last time I slept, let alone slept in? She does something to me. Something I can't explain. But if I don't get her back, I will die. I don't want to be alive in a life where she doesn't exist."

"Rob, man, you're scaring me."

"You should be fucking scared. I'm fucking pissed. This is Lizzie all over again. What if we don't make it in time? What if I never find her?"

"Calm down. I will grab my gear, get the jet, and be there in two hours," Tony replied, trying to calm his agitated friend.

Rob ran a hand roughly over his face and through his hair. He stopped on the back of his neck and rubbed it, trying to calm himself. His voiced wavered as he spoke. "I can't lose her, man."

"Oh no! Not you, too," Tony quipped. "What the fuck is going on around here. I heard those exact same words from Michael about one year ago."

"You don't understand. I will explain it to you when you get here. You've met her. You've seen her. I can't let her go," Rob explained. "Not after last night."

"Why? What happened last night?"

Rob spoke too much. He was just so used to sharing everything with Tony and Michael. They were his brothers.

In his most reassuring voice, Tony said, "We will get her, man. We found her once; we will find her again. She was wearing the necklace, right?"

"I am going to find her or die trying." There, he said it to his friend. "There is no coming back for me this time if we don't find her." There would be no sugarcoating this. Rob was all in on this, his most important mission. This time there was no one else to worry about, just his Lola. He had to find her. He would find her. It was twisted in his mind, but saving Lola would make up for not saving Lizzie. He knew he was good at what he did. He was a good solider.

"Don't talk like that, man. I didn't realize this girl meant so much to you," Tony cautioned his friend, trying to bring him back to reality.

"Don't say shit like that to me. She is my everything! She is my world. I will not lose her, do you understand? If you aren't ready to die, I can do this without you. But know this, I am not leaving without her."

"I get it, man. I didn't realize. I'm sorry. You know I have your back. I will be right there beside you when we find her."

"Thank you," Rob said. He needed his friend's steady confidence and strength just like he needed it when Lizzie died. He needed Tony, Michael, and Steve now more than ever. He could still save her. No one was torturing her, yet. No one was raping her, yet. They wanted to sell her so they would keep her in good condition. That gave him a morsel of comfort. He just had to find them in time.

Rob ran upstairs to the guest room and shoved his shirt and pants into his gear bag. He hurried to Lola's room and grabbed some of her stuff and shoved it into his gear bag as well. When he was ready, he jumped into his rented SUV and drove to the airfield where he waited for Tony to appear. A little over an hour later, Tony landed and disembarked the plane. It would need more fuel. He walked in to ask the controller to have it refueled when he spotted Rob. Rob's head hung low and his shoulders slumped. Tony hurried over to Rob and extended his hand. Without hesitation, Rob grabbed his brother's hand and hugged him with his other arm. The two men embraced until Rob pulled away. Tony was there for him.

"You realize we might die this time?" Rob offered.

"I know. I'm ready. I already talked to Steve. You know he's in."

"What about Tyrrell? Did you tell him?"

"I only told him it was an emergency. He's waiting to be debriefed when we return," Tony warned his friend.

"We don't have time for a debriefing. He's either going to trust me or he isn't. But I do need his resources," Rob admitted.

"Then bring him in. He has always had our backs in the past. He will have them again, especially since he is still on Richard Sardeson's payroll," Tony promised.

After the agonizing thirty minutes it took to refuel the plane and pay the controller, they were finally taxiing down the runway.

They pulled up to the office building of Blackrain Security, grabbed their gear bags from the backseat, and ran into the building. The Ortiz Cartel now had a half day start on them. Rob went straight to Tyrrell's office.

"What's the emergency?" Tyrrell questioned.

"We don't have a lot of time. The Ortiz Cartel recaptured Lola, and it's my fault. I was there and didn't stop it."

"Did you see it happen? Why didn't you go after them?"

Rob hung his head in shame and mumbled, "I was sleeping."

"You're kidding?" Tyrrell knew him better than that. Hell, anyone who knew Rob knew he didn't sleep, yet alone soundly.

"Look, I already know I fucked up. Now I need your help to fix it. Can I count on you?" Rob asked, cutting to the chase.

"You have worked for me for a little under a year. Have I ever let you down? What makes you think I would now?"

"This is a do or die mission for me. Are you still in?"

"What do you need? You're lead," Tyrrell reassured him.

"I need a satellite location on the Ortiz Cartel. Pull up Lola's necklace GPS. Call the FBI, the CIA, whomever you need to call. Hell, call them all. I need authorization to take down the entire Cartel. No man left standing. I won't leave a man alive. Lola isn't safe until all of those motherfuckers are in the ground. You still in?" Rob asked with a worried voice.

"Explain to me why you are willing to risk your life and the life of my men for a woman you just met. You aren't even being paid for this mission," Tyrrell said as he raised a brow quizzically.

"I can't explain it because I don't understand it myself, but Lola has done something to me. I'm hers as long as she will have me. And I promised her no harm would come to her. I intend to keep that promise."

"You're talking about taking down an entire drug cartel for one woman," Tyrrell argued.

"I know exactly what I'm doing. And I am doing this. I know Tony and Steve will be in with me. The only question is, will you?"

"You're going to need more help than that. I need to reach out to my contacts with the FBI and let them know about this. And what are you going to do if you get caught? At most this will be an unsanctioned mission. You know damn well the FBI can't move on a Mexican cartel located in Mexico."

"I know that. I'm not blind, nor am I stupid. But I won't let anything happen to Lola. She's already been taken. I have to get to her before they sell her again or worse."

"Do you love her?" Tyrrell asked, pretty sure of the answer.

"Yes," Rob responded. "She has me, boss. When I'm with her, I'm alive again. The memory of Lizzie's death stops playing in my head. She brought me back to life. And I'll be damned if I don't get her back. I will do whatever is necessary for her."

"I didn't realize you could feel so strongly after only a few days."

"I knew it the minute I saw her. I knew I had to have her. She was more than a mission from the second I laid eyes on her. She feels it, too. I'm not crazy. We're both unique individuals. It just happened fast for us. So what do you say? Do I have your support?" Rob asked, hope filling his eyes.

"Let me make a few phone calls then we will talk strategy."

Rob extended his hand and Tyrrell shook it, looking at him with both eyes. Tyrrell could see the fire and love that burned in Rob's eyes. He would be the last person to extinguish it. And hell, even Tyrrell knew if anything happened to Lola, Rob would go over the cliff never to return.

Rob met Tyrrell's steady eyes. "I am in love with her." He turned and walked out of the room. There was nothing left to say. That one sentence summed up everything for Rob. He loved her with his entire being. He would figure a way to let Lizzie go after he got Lola back. He still didn't know how he could love her after Lizzie, but that was how he felt. He would die for her. And one only dies for true love.

STRONGER

It took the better part of the morning, but Tony had pinpointed the Ortiz Cartel to within a one-mile radius. Ortiz's compound was large. Satellite imagery showed a main house, several outlying smaller structures, and one large warehouse. The warehouse must be where he got his drugs ready for distribution. Satellite imagery also showed large trucks moving in and out of the compound. The trucks backed up to the warehouse for loading, so it had to have a loading dock.

The main house was large. They would need to get boots on the ground to stake out the compound and study the armed guards and their movements. A stakeout like this could take two weeks. Tony just hoped Rob didn't lose his shit during that time. He didn't know how he was going to keep his brother from going on a suicide mission. They had to make this a clean takedown. They would eliminate the Ortiz Cartel so they could never sell another innocent girl ever again.

The next morning, Tony awoke from a fitful sleep in one of the bedrooms housed at Blackrain's office building. The room didn't have a window, so he had no idea what time it was until he glanced at the clock on the side of the table: 0627. Getting out of bed, he headed to the shower. He thought about the right words to say to Rob that would calm him down and make him wait the required length of time necessary to track Ortiz's men's movements. There could be no mistakes. This operation had to go off without a hitch.

Tony knew Tyrrell spent the better part of the evening contacting everyone he knew in all law enforcement agencies and would have information for them today. Tony was anxious to hear that information. Having the FBI backing their mission meant they didn't go to jail. That was important to Tony. After five tours in Afghanistan, he rather liked his freedom.

He quickly lathered his body with soap and rinsed. He stepped from the hot shower with red marks on his back from where the hot water had washed away his guilt for the day. Tony had seen and done many things he wasn't proud of; things that weighed on his conscious like a load of cinder blocks. He didn't suffer from the nightmares like his brothers did. Now that Michael had Emma, Michael told him his nightmares had dissipated, but Tony knew Rob and Steve suffered from them nightly. They often confided in him about what they constantly dreamt about, and they were the same things that weighed on Tony's mind: the killings, the close brushes with death they'd each had, the torture they inflicted on other human beings, the kill or be killed mindset which they were all still living with. These thoughts plagued Tony's mind as they did the minds off all the men in The Unit.

He stepped from the shower, dried himself off, and quickly dressed. He ambled down the hallway to the conference room to find an anguish-filled Rob, Tyrrell, Steve, and Aaron waiting on him.

"Nice of you to join us," Tyrrell commented, tapping his watch.

"I didn't realize we were scheduled to meet this morning," Tony replied. "I came to brief you on what I found last night."

"Great, we will get to that in a second. First, I want to go over how this will play out," Tyrrell said, looking Rob directly in the eyes. "We will stake out the compound until we are certain we have the routine of Ortiz and his men down pat. We will not enter the compound until we can say, without a doubt, where subject one will be and when. These men have a routine, and they will stick to it. Spend enough time watching and yes, waiting, to figure it out. I just got off the phone with the FBI. They can't officially support this mission and will deny knowing anything about it. But they are willing to go along with it after the man you turned over to them a week or so ago confirmed they are running a sex-slave trade and abducting girls from the United States. They can't send a team, but they will keep us out of hot water. That is, as long as we don't get caught."

"We, boss? I thought I was leading this mission with Michael being gone," Rob inquired.

"You are. But I will be a member of that team. It's been a while since I have been out in the field, and God knows, you're going to need all the help you can get.

We will have a five-man team. You, Tony, Steve, Aaron, and myself."

The men looked to each other. Tyrrell coming out on a mission. None of the men had ever been in combat with him before. Could they trust him with their lives, with Lola's life?

"I was a Navy SEAL. The best. I have kept up with my training. I'll have your backs," Tyrrell said, catching the look of uncertainty in The Unit's eyes.

Rob sat, bouncing his leg up and down under the table so hard, the coffee was moving. He tugged on the collar of his t-shirt. Finally, unable to wait any longer, Rob stood quickly and knocked over his cup of coffee. "Sorry, boss, I'll get it…I'll clean it up." Rob reentered the room with a handful of paper towels. "When do we leave?" Rob questioned as he cleared his throat and sopped up the mess on the table.

"Gather your things and be ready for takeoff at 1300." Tyrrell grabbed Rob's hand and stopped his frantic movements, which were just sloshing the coffee all over the table. He squeezed Rob's hand, and he let go of the paper towels. Tyrrell finished cleaning up the mess then he turned to face his men who were now standing beside his office door. "Go, get ready. This is going to be a long mission. Prepare. Make your phone calls. Be ready at 1300." He dismissed the men with a wave of his hand and threw the sopping wet paper towels into the trash can.

Rob was the first out of the door. At his locker, he grabbed his Sig 226, his Glock 19, his Walther P22, and his knife. He glanced over at Tony and the man was filling his gear bag with tactical assault rifles, including his 240 Bravo—a favorite of his from his time in the Army.

Once the gear bags were loaded, they studied the satellite imagery Tony had gathered from the FBI satellites. Tony went over the compound with The Unit and covered the most likely places to have guards stationed. Rob paced and cursed the entire time, trying to wait for 1300. Finally, they were loading into the SUV which would take them to the airfield.

They grabbed their gear bags from the SUV and loaded into the private jet set to land on the same airstrip as the first mission. Finally, slouching down in his seat, Rob felt he was getting started. The plane was going to touch down, and he was going in. He had to find Lola.

STRONGER

CHAPTER
TWENTY-THREE

Lola lay on her lumpy cot mattress thankful they weren't feeding her drugs this time. They wanted to give her every chance to think about the upcoming sale. She hadn't heard mention of when it was going to be, but this time was different. Not only were they not feeding her pills, they also had her in a hut by herself. She wasn't examined after the initial two day period like she was the first time. But it was the same type of hut, so she knew she was back in the same place. The same type of bucket sat in the corner.

She slowly rolled over, stretching her body. She had slept fitfully all night. She awoke every hour or so with the thought of a rescue she was beginning to think would never come. She picked up the rock and marked her tenth mark into the packed dirt floor of the hut. In that time, no one had come to talk to her or do anything with her but change her bucket and bring her food. She noticed her food wasn't as good as last time. Maybe that was the effect of not being high on the pills they fed her before. Over the last day or two, she didn't really have an appetite. Smells made her nauseous. That bucket in the corner was doing a number on her. She was so sensitive to it, she could pick up the urine and feces smell even after she placed the lid back on it. She was nauseous, and she was sure it was her nerves. Unlike last time, this time she knew exactly what they wanted from her. Only this time she wasn't a virgin.

What would they do to her when they found out? Surely the doctor would examine her again. Would they still sell her? Of course they would. They only cared about one thing: money. They would sell her to the highest bidder. Now she wished she wasn't as pretty as she was. If she were unattractive, they would have probably never have taken her in the first place. She wasn't vain, just honest. She knew men found her attractive; it was apparent each time she entered a club or danced in one. They flocked to her like sheep to their shepherd. She had been so bold before, playing up her looks to torment and tease. Now she regretted teasing the men the way she had. Karma was a bitch, and she was getting hers.

She wondered about Rob. What was he doing over the last ten days? Was he trying to find her? Her gut told her yes. He felt something for her, of that she was certain. It couldn't be one-sided. Feelings as strong as hers had to be shared. She knew he would be blaming himself for her being taken again. He had blamed himself for not saving Lizzie, so it would only stand to reason that he blamed himself for her predicament, too. Would he get to her in time? Would she be forced through the degrading process of prancing around in front of the men who sat behind the mirrors again? Would someone who meant to do her harm buy her this time?

She couldn't do it. She couldn't live under a man's thumb. If Rob did save her, the first thing she would do would be to kiss him. The second thing would be to have a serious conversation about him considering her a possession. That would never work for her. She had to be free. Free to go where she pleased and free to befriend whom she pleased.

Rob. She missed him something terrible. While it was true they only knew each other a short time, she still felt feelings for him that were so strong, so potent, the thought of not seeing him again had her in tears.

She sat against the bamboo wall of the hut, shoulders slumped as she covered her face. What good did it do her to cry? She had to be ready for what the Cartel would do. Still, she wrapped her arms around herself. She would be brave. Rob would want her to be brave. She would face what was to come alone. She knew she had to mentally prepare herself. She knew in her heart Rob was working on rescuing her. But just in case he didn't make it in time, she had to be brave.

Just then the door to her hut opened and in walked an armed guard. She jumped at the chance to talk to him, for some sort of connection to the outside world.

"What day is it?" she asked.

"Wednesday. The doctor will come for you in a few hours," the man said while walking over to her bucket and grabbing it by the handle.

"Wait. Can't you stay and talk to me. I have been alone for so long. I just want to know what you have planned for me."

One could tell the man felt sorry for her, yet he kept his gun readied in his hand. He would shoot her if she tried anything. Maybe she could seduce information out of him. Men had always responded to her before, what would make this man any different. She jumped from the bed and caught him gently by the arm before he had a chance to exit the hut. "Am I going to be sold again?" she asked, already knowing the answer. She left her hand on his skin, which burned under her touch. He turned to face her, his mouth drawn into a tight line. She could tell he didn't like his job. The thought of selling her did something to him. He tightened his grip on his gun as she let her hand trail its way down his arm gently and fall away.

"I shouldn't be talking to you. You are merchandise, nothing more." He shook his head. He opened his mouth as if to speak, only to close it again.

"Tell me, how many of us are there? How many girls will be sold this time?"

He pulled his brows inward and looked down at the ground. He took a deep breath and then exhaled in a rush. Telling her this information could get him shot. He raised his head and made eye contact.

She could see the conflict warring inside his mind. He rubbed his hand over his heart. "Why do you want to know? Won't that just make it harder for you?" he questioned.

"Please." She stepped closer to him. He inhaled her scent deep into his lungs. He had never smelled anything or anyone who smelled so good. Surely this was an angel sent by God. What if he did tell her?

What would she do with the information? Who could she tell? She was kept here, in this hut, guarded. What if Ortiz found him talking to her? What would Ortiz do to him? They were to be merchandise and that was all, much like the drugs.

Finally he let out a long, slow sigh. He would give her this information. He would help this angel in any way he could. Still, he could never go up against the Ortiz Cartel; he was but one man.

"There are fifteen of you."

Fifteen young, innocent girls. Last time there had been twelve besides her. She had to stop this, but how? She was but one woman.

"When is the auction scheduled? How long do I have?" she asked, backing away from the bearer of bad news. He let his gun hang from his shoulder strap as he reached out his hand to bring her chin up to meet his eyes.

"It will happen in one week. Arrangements and invitations have already been sent."

She had one week of freedom left. Rob had one week or he would lose her forever. She knew if Rob lost her, he would never again find himself. She stumbled forward as she tried to walk and fell into the man. The man grabbed her with his free hand and spilled some of the contents of the bucket onto the floor.

Clutching her stomach, Lola indicated she was going to be sick. She darted to the corner, away from her cot, and retched up the contents of her stomach. She was ill at the thought of Rob never finding her. Ill at the thought of never being in Rob's arms again. Ill at the thought of belonging to a man who purchased her.

When she was done throwing up, she wiped her mouth with the back of her hand. She had no way to brush her teeth, and now she was going to have to live with the smell of vomit for the next week.

"Do you think…I mean, is there any way you could get me something to clean that up with?" She motioned to the vomit.

The man, standing there watching her helplessly, nodded his head. "I will be back with your empty bucket and a towel. But you mustn't tell anyone where you got it from. I could die for helping you."

She walked to the man closing the distance in five paces. She touched his cheek and again felt his skin burn beneath her touch. "Are you sick?" she asked, concerned about the man who agreed to help her.

"No. I'm fine. Thank you for your concern." He had to get out of there. She was doing something to him, softening him in a world that only punished that quality.

He turned to leave her, and her hand fell to her side. She had found an ally she could use. Would she have occasion to use him?

A short time later the man returned with an empty bucket and a towel just like he said he would. She got up from the cot and greeted him in the middle of the hut. "Thank you for your kindness," she whispered so only he could hear. "I have another question," she whispered.

"What is it?"

"What day next week will I be sold?" She watched as the man's face went hard. His expression was now unreadable. He masked his feelings quite well. She had no idea if she had made him angry or repentant.

"Next Friday. You have about ten days left."

"And I will not receive drugs during this time?" she inquired, hoping they would not give her any. She needed a clear head to come up with a plan.

"No drugs. Not for you. They want you to suffer for escaping them and ruining their sale of you last time," he confided. "With no drugs and no others in your hut, you are forced into isolation with nothing but time to think about what is coming." He bowed his head and stared at his dusty boots.

She was thankful they sought to punish her. She did not want the drugs again, although it would be nice not to care, but it was now up to her to figure a way out of this. She had asked for and received the help of one guard. Would he be enough?

"Tell me, how many men guard me?" she pushed, hoping his kindness would continue.

"I have said enough to get me killed. I can't answer any more of your questions."

"I understand," she acquiesced under the stare of a man who really was afraid for his life. She threw herself into him and hugged him. He stood stiff and erect, unused to the affection of the merchandise, especially one so beautiful. "Thank you for the towel," she said as she reached to take it from his hand. She approached the corner with a lump rising in the back of her throat. As she knelt to clean up the mess, she started to gag.

He touched her shoulder. "Here, let me," he said as he reached down and took the towel from her small hand.

"Thank you." She stood and walked to the other side of the room. She would surely vomit again over the smell.

When the man finished picking up the vomit, he walked to the door of the hut. He turned to look at Lola sitting on the cot. "I'm sorry," he said, then he turned and exited through the door.

An RV camper that housed the mobile
surveillance headquarters for The Unit blended in
perfectly with the wealthier area of Mexico. Inside the
RV, The Unit took care to outfit it with the latest in
technology. The antenna looked like a regular
television antenna, but it was really used to monitor
satellite feed. There were several computers for display
of the satellite feed. They used this feed to monitor and
track the activity of the Ortiz Cartel. It was important
for this mission that they kept close enough to the Ortiz
compound but far enough away as to not alert any nosy
neighbors to their business. It was for that reason they
moved the camper every few days. The camper's
windows were lined with heavy opaque curtains so
they could see out, but nobody could see in. The
camper had enough room for sleeping quarters for the
five men. The bathroom was cramped, but it served its
purpose. There was a partition which separated the
driver and passenger seats from the rest of the RV.
Inside, they had stocked the camper with enough food
and water to last three weeks. They weren't sure they
would be in the camper for that length of time but had
to take every precaution. They couldn't risk being

seen. They had to be very careful about the noise level as it had to appear as if the RV was unoccupied, and they had to be cautious of their movements. If they rocked the camper, it could give away their hiding spot.

Their plan was to keep the RV parked in a shopping center parking lot, rotating between the three in the area so they could remain invisible. They had stocked the van with all the weapons they would need to take down the Ortiz Cartel, but each man was starting to grate on each other's nerves. Spending a lot of time in close quarters was par for the course in the military, so this was nothing new to them. Everyone, with the exception of Tyrrell, served in the Army and served in one or more of the wars the United States were engaged in over the last decade. Tyrrell was a Navy SEAL. He wasn't used to surveillance. He was used to action. He was growing more annoyed by the minute.

Rob sat motionless in one of the leather seats inside the RV. He could not stand himself. His shoulders were slumped and his hands lay limply in his lap. He had failed Lizzie, and now he had failed Lola. Thoughts of Lizzie grunting and screaming entered his mind. He was racked with guilt. In the next breath, his thoughts turned to Lola. He still could feel her touch. He could still smell her unique scent. He could still feel her lips pressed against his. His body started to tremble. Thoughts of losing Lola took over. Thoughts of finding her dead, just like he found Lizzie, clouded his judgment.

He begged God. "Please, God. Let me save her. Let me be the one to rescue her. I know I failed Lizzie, but if I could rescue Lola, it would somehow start to make up for not saving Lizzie. I'll never forget Lizzie, and I'll always carry the guilt, but at least I will have saved Lola. I know you don't owe me anything because of the sins I have committed, albeit for the greater good, but sins nonetheless. I have taken the lives of men, bad men, but I still killed them. Please forgive me, Father, and please give me the strength and the wisdom to save Lola." As he said his prayer, he swiveled his captain's chair away from the other men in the camper. He did not want them to see him in his current state. The shame of Lola being taken right from under his nose was too much to bear.

After a few minutes, his muscles began clenching along his jawline. He had a headache he would ignore for the sake of this mission. He had to think of it as a mission and detach himself from Lola if he could. If his emotions clouded his judgment, they would both be lost. He moved into Tony's space in the back of the cramped RV. They had been staking out the Ortiz Cartel from a distance using the best money could buy for two weeks. They had the routines of Ortiz's men down. The only thing they didn't know was when the auction would be held. They hadn't sensed any movement in regards to the girls and women located in the huts. They had caught a glimpse of the women as they were led into the mansion on the property, but he had yet to visually confirm Lola's presence.

"Have you seen her yet?" Rob asked Tony in a clipped tone. The GPS chip in her necklace confirmed her location, but Rob wanted visual confirmation.

"Not yet, but think of all the other girls we are saving besides Lola. There must be fifteen girls up for auction," Tony reminded his friend.

"Let's go over it one more time."

"Okay. We have two armed guards here." Tony pointed to the computer monitor showing two men stationed outside the large warehouse on the property. "This," Tony said, motioning to the warehouse, "must be where they keep their drugs and ready them for distribution."

"How many men and women have you seen enter and exit that building daily?"

"There are about twenty civilians working in the warehouse. "Here are the four roving guards," Tony continued, pointing to the four men currently meeting under a tree talking and smoking.

"How many men are on the huts?" Rob questioned.

"Two, as far as I can tell. Look at how close the huts are to one another. Two men can easily guard fifteen scared women and children. Didn't Lola say Ortiz kept them drugged?"

"Yes. She said that when she was on the drug, she didn't care who or where she was, as long as she was given more."

"Here," Tony said, pointing to the mansion, "are two armed guards at the front door to the mansion. And every time I have seen Ortiz, he has been alone. He obviously feels confident his security is enough to keep him safe on his grounds."

Rob looked at the men in the back of the van. He knew two of them better than he knew himself. The variables were Aaron and Tyrrell. He had no choice but to trust them with his life as they would trust Rob with theirs.

Rob met Tyrrell's eyes. "Here's what we are going to do."

After Rob laid out the plan, each man started to make their way to their gear bags. They armed each weapon and placed silencers on their Walther P22's. These guns were perfect for a mission like this. A Walther P22 with a silencer made one noise—the scraping of metal on metal. There was no crack, just the action slide. If they were going to pull off this operation, they had to be as silent as possible. They were outnumbered twelve to five. However, Rob was certain their training made up for the fact that Ortiz had more men on the ground.

Tony pulled out two dowels and a length of medium gauge piano wire. He set to the task of making a garrote. He drilled one hole in each dowel and threaded the piano wire through the hole. He then wrapped the wire around itself to secure its attachment to the dowel. Piano wire stretched and attached to the dowels, one on each side, made for the perfect weapon for choking a subject. The piano wire cut as it strangled. There would be gurgling noises as the subject choked on his own blood. He may not need it with the suppressed firepower they were carrying, but he wanted to cover all bases.

Aaron and Steve were cleaning their sniper rifles as they readied for battle. Soon, they would be taking down a notorious drug cartel. They prayed everything would go as planned. The FBI considered this an unsanctioned mission. They could not be caught nor captured or they would die in Mexico with no one coming to save them, no reinforcements. The Unit was the only chance these women and girls had of being rescued in time.

Tyrrell was on his cell phone gathering intelligence when Rob approached. "Sure. Thank you, sir." Tyrrell pressed the end button.

"What's up? What have you learned?" Rob questioned.

"They are moving the girls on Friday."

"This Friday?" Rob asked, clenching his fists at his side.

"This Friday. We have five days. We have our plan. We have our weapons. We know our jobs. We will take them down," Tyrrell reassured Rob.

"I just hope we don't lose in the process," Rob said as his thoughts once again drifted to Lola.

Lola looked over the side of her cot and down at the ground. She had marked the days until the auction, and each day she would put a mark through the day as a countdown. She had two days until she was sold and still no Rob. *Where was he?* She felt certain he was out there and he was going to rescue her, but the closer it came to the day, the more anxious she became.

She was always nauseous now. It must have been her nerves. The first time she had pills. This time she was left alone with her mind.

She missed Rob. She missed his strong hands on her stomach. She missed his caress of her face. She missed his rough touch brushing against her soft skin. Finding herself thinking of him constantly, she shook it off. She had to come up with a plan in case he couldn't find her in time. What if she became someone's property? How would she survive? Would Rob continue to look for her until he found her and saved her again? All these questions left unanswered in her mind.

Her friend was back: the man who brought her the towel and continued to clean up the subsequent vomit. She had been throwing up at least twice a day. It had to be her nerves. But nerves wouldn't explain her heightened sense of smell. She could smell everything. It was unnatural to smell that well.

Her friend walked to the corner and began gathering the vomit into the towel. He would make it as bearable as possible for her while she was here.

"The doctor is coming later today," he told her as he shook out the towel in the bucket.

"Will it be the same as last time?"

"Yes. He will examine you to make sure you are still a virgin."

Oh no! She didn't think about that. She was no longer a virgin. What would they do with her when they found out? Would they still sell her? They had to. They sold Dangani, Cece, and Alisha, and two of them weren't virgins. She just wouldn't be wearing white. They could still make a profit off of her. She knew she was attractive. She knew men wanted her. Someone would buy her. Surely they had to sell her. All they cared about was money.

"When will he come to examine me?" Lola asked, trying to prepare herself for the debasement to come.

"This evening. He is examining all of the girls today. The man to choose your clothes will be here afterwards."

She was thankful for this bit of information. However, that meant that she would come face-to-face with the bald, fat man who tried to take advantage of her. The man who smelled of alcohol and cigars. The memory of that incident made her even more nauseous.

She stood from the cot and walked over to meet the man at the bucket. She recoiled from the strong odor and took a few steps back. He reached out and placed his hand on her arm to steady her. She felt faint. Maybe she got up too fast. She felt her knees go weak and then everything faded to black.

She awoke on her cot. The nice man was gone. She could tell from the sun's position through the crack between the roof and the wall that it was late in the afternoon. She must have passed out from all of the stress.

She was right about the time because a little while later the nice man came back with her dinner of chicken, rice, and carrots. They did make sure she was well fed; she would give Ortiz that. She was famished. She ate every last bite of her dinner and placed the empty plate back on the floor. She drank the entire glass of water he brought and placed it next to the plate. As of late, the only time she could eat was in the evenings. She couldn't touch her breakfast or lunch. Just the thought of food while she was so nauseous made it so much worse.

The nice man entered her room to remove her dinner dishes.

"I'm scared," she confessed to the man.

"I'm truly sorry. I don't like what they do, but I have no choice but to do my job. They pay well, and I have a large family that depends on the money."

She nodded, pretending to understand. Still she couldn't fathom how such a kind man could stand guard with a gun strapped to his shoulder ready to shoot anyone who got out of line. Would he shoot her?

"Would you shoot me?" she wondered aloud.

"If I was ordered to, yes."

His words scared her even more. He didn't really care about her if he could kill her based on an order. But it was true, if he disobeyed, more than likely he would be killed and so would his family. She had heard Rob talk with Tony about the Ortiz Cartel, and what she heard scared her even more.

The Ortiz Cartel was a ruthless cartel smuggling drugs into the United States and selling innocent girls and women, who they kidnapped from all over the world, into slavery. God, they must have scouts in every major city. Ortiz was a powerful man. She was sure he killed anyone who didn't comply with his wishes. It still perplexed her about the nice man who would kill her. He wouldn't help her escape, but she had to try.

She walked seductively to him, swaying her hips slightly and pushing her breasts out, standing straight. She flung her long hair over her shoulder and brought her hand to it. She took a strand of her hair and started to twirl it around her finger while she looked directly into the man's kind brown eyes. "Would you help me?"

"How?" the man asked, considering helping the gorgeous creature before him.

"Can you get me out of here before the doctor comes?"

The man backed away from her as if her presence was a strong fire giving off heat too hot to stand next to. He didn't want to get smoke in his eyes. When he was next to the door, he spoke. "I am sorry. I can't help you. They know where my family lives."

She lowered her head in defeat and whispered, "I understand." And she did understand. She didn't want anything to happen to this man's family. This man who had been nothing but kind to her. The man apologized again and left, carrying the dinner dishes, through the door.

When the sun had set, the doctor came in to visit her. "Ah, so we meet again," he said, his lips curling into an evil smile. "Take off your bottoms and your underwear."

Lola unbuttoned her shorts and hooked her thumbs into her panties and shorts and pulled them down her legs. She stepped out of the garments and stood exposed before the man.

"Lie down and spread your legs," he said clinically.

Lola sat on her cot and laid back. Embarrassed and ashamed, she let her knees fall to the sides until she was laid vulnerably open before the doctor. The doctor put on a pair of latex gloves, pulled out the tube of jelly, and squirted some on his fingers. He pressed into her opening and then froze. He looked down at her and met her eyes. "You're no longer a virgin?" It sounded like a question, but it was more of a statement. "I will have to inform Senor Ortiz. He will not be pleased." He smiled his evil grin as he said it. Weren't doctors supposed to swear an oath to uphold ethical standards? What the hell was ethical about examining women and girls in the manner in which he did?

"What will happen now?" Lola mumbled, afraid of the answer.

"I will talk to Senor Ortiz and get back to you."

The doctor took care to remove his gloves stuffing one inside of the other so the side that touched his hands was now on the outside and the jelly side was inside. He placed the used gloves in his bag and left the hut.

An hour or so passed and now no light shone in the room from outside. It was completely dark. She couldn't determine the time, but she was extremely tired. She laid on her cot to sleep.

"Wake up!"

She felt a nudging at her knee. She opened her eyes and saw Ortiz and the doctor standing over her. She flinched into herself, afraid of Ortiz. She sank as far into the mattress as possible.

"You're no longer a virgin. You just cost me two hundred grand you little bitch. I hope it was worth it," Ortiz spat as he grabbed hold of her hair and forced her to sit up. He turned to the doctor. "Do the test."

The doctor reached into his bag and pulled out a cup. He thrust it to Lola and said, "Go pee in this."

Ortiz pulled her to a standing position by her hair. She clutched the cup to her bosom with both hands. What kind of test could they possibly be running? She was led to the bucket and told to pee again. She pulled her shorts and panties down to her knees and squatted over the bucket, placing the cup where she expected her urine stream to be. She tried but couldn't pee with them watching her.

Mustering all of her courage, she said, "If you want me to pee in this cup, you're going to have to leave. I can't do it with you here."

"We aren't leaving, so you better figure out a way."

"Will you at least turn around?" she asked quietly.

The men turned their backs to her, and she did her best to block them out. After a few minutes of willing her body to pee, she finally did. She filled the cup half full and set it on the ground. She pulled up her panties and shorts. "All done," she said as she picked the cup up from the floor.

The doctor walked to her with his arm outstretched. She handed him the cup. He walked back to his bag and pulled out a stick which he then unwrapped and dipped in the urine. Both men focused intently on the stick.

She felt the air in the room change. Something bad was going to happen as Ortiz's eyes met hers. He stalked to her, raised his hand and, without warning, backhanded her, knocking her to the ground. She sat on the ground supported by her hand with her other hand held firmly against her cheek to push against the pain. She looked up at him. "What's wrong?" she asked, knowing whatever it was wasn't good for her.

"You're pregnant, you bitch." He reached down and grabbed a handful of her hair and dragged her to a kneeling position facing the back of the hut. "Guard,"

Ortiz bellowed into the night. The nice man came running into the hut.

"Yes, senor."

"Kill her." Ortiz moved to the side of the hut to watch this bitch, who cost him over three hundred grand, die.

The doctor stepped to the other side of the cabin, a sick grin upon his face. She prayed like she never prayed in her life. She was pregnant with Rob's baby. She was never going to get the life she always wanted. Rob's baby. For the briefest of moments, she allowed herself the happiness of the knowledge that she carried Rob's baby. Rob's baby. If only she could find a way out of this, she could finally have the life she always dreamed of. Being a mother and a wife. But she was going to die. Worse, her baby was going to die. She moved her hands in a protective gesture to cover her belly. She clenched her eyes shut as tears streamed down her face. "Please," she begged, but she wasn't sure if she was begging God or Ortiz who were one in the same at that moment.

She braced herself as she felt the handgun pressed against the back of her head. She squeezed her eyes closed tighter. At least it would be quick. She heard the click of the trigger as the sound of a single gunshot erupted into the room.

Rob and his team stood on the perimeter of the Ortiz compound. The tropical forest surrounding it provided the perfect cover for The Unit.

"Steve and Aaron, you guys get sniper eyes on the guards in the compound. Take up positions there and there," Rob said, pointing the highest locations in the forest. From the chosen locations, Steve and Aaron would not be able to cover the entire compound, just the main courtyard. It would have to do. Their thermal optics always came in handy for nighttime missions.

"Tony and Tyrrell, you are on my six. We will take out as many as we can as quietly as possible. No noise. No one knows we're here. Let's keep it that way."

Steve and Aaron disappeared deeper into the forest. Night provided the perfect cover. The armed guards would never know what hit them. They could easily sneak up on the subject and take him out. Rob, Tony, and Tyrrell moved in the shadows of the forest until it was time to climb the barbed wire fence. There was no way to avoid it as it surrounded the compound. They scaled the fence with efficiency and placed the piece of carpet they were carrying over the barbed wire, leaving the carpet behind. Once on the ground, they were hidden by several huts that lined the west side of the property. Clearing the fence was their first hurdle; it was now time to split up. The plan was to take out the four roving guards before taking out the warehouse guards. Next they would take out the guards on the mansion, and lastly, they would take out the guards guarding the hut.

Tony was the first to come across an armed roving guard. He quietly moved behind the man until he was standing directly behind him. With speed and accuracy, Tony gripped the man's head with his left hand and quickly wrapped the piano wire around the man's neck under his chin. Tony used the dowels to pull taut on the wire, effectively strangling him. The man struggled and kicked, but Tony was prepared. He had him in a death lock. The piano wire was doing its job. Two minutes later, Tony placed the man softly to the ground and moved to find his next victim.

Rob found a roving guard under a tree smoking a cigarette. Little did he know it would be his last. Rob crept up behind him and in one swift move, snapped the man's neck. Silence. No shots fired yet.

They continued in this fashion, taking out the four roving guards. The men guarding the warehouse and the mansion would be harder. They would need their Walther P22's for this. Rob walked in the darkness until he stood 100 yards in front of the guards at the warehouse. He moved behind a tree for cover and knelt on the ground to aim his gun at subject one's head. Silently, the man fell to his death. He fired another shot quickly before the second man had a chance to react. The sound of metal scraping metal was the only sound heard as he fired the second shot. He hit the man right between the eyes. The armed guard fell silently. He hoped Tony and Tyrrell were having the same luck.

Tyrrell let Tony take aim at one of the guards from the mansion. Tony hit the man in the chest and he fell to the ground, but he wasn't dead. Tony could see the man moving. The second guard on the mansion was on alert, but before he had a chance to radio, Steve took him out with his sniper rifle. Tyrrell and Tony ran to the steps of the mansion in the cover of darkness. They needed to be quick. There was a light shining on the wounded man from the mansion. Tyrrell pulled his knife and stabbed the man in the chest piercing his lung. He pulled the knife from the man and, with extreme quickness, plunged the knife back into the man's heart. Blood covered his hand, but the man was now dead. Now they only had the armed guards on the rear doors of the mansion and on the huts to worry about.

Tyrrell and Tony moved stealthily along the side wall of the mansion. Tony peeked around the corner and spotted the guards on the patio. Tony held his hand up for Tyrrell, and he followed Tony around the side of the mansion crouched low to the ground. The guards were standing and talking. There was no way to take a shot. They had to create a distraction to get the guards to come down the steps. Tony looked down and saw a landscaping rock. He picked it up and threw it over his shoulder into the yard. It landed but didn't hit the tree that he aimed for. He picked up another rock and aimed at the tree. He released the rock, and it sailed through the air, knocking against the tree. The guards fell silent and readied their weapons. One of the guards called into his radio about possible movement on the grounds. This is exactly what The Unit didn't need.

With lightning speed, the guards moved down the steps and split up. They were going to flank the area the noise had come from. As soon as they moved into the backyard, Tony and Tyrrell moved into position behind them. Tony pulled his Walther P22 and aimed it at the man's head. All that could be heard was the action slide as Tony fired his shot. The man dropped to the ground. The other guard heard the man drop and rushed to his body. Tyrrell carefully approached as the man raised his walkie-talkie to his mouth. Before the guard could alert the others, Tyrrell placed his right arm around the man' s neck and locked the choke hold into position by gripping his left arm with his right hand. He brought his left hand up and used it to press down against the man's head. Once the man was in the chokehold, Tyrrell squeezed his muscles as tight as he could, effectually strangling the man. The man must have been trained, because he brought both of his hands up and clawed at Tyrrell's arm that was under his chin. The guard tucked his hands in between his neck and Tyrrell's arm. The guard widened his stance and squatted. He tucked his chin into the space his hands afforded him. Using his left hand, the guard threw off Tyrrell's left arm, breaking the chokehold. The guard pulled down on Tyrrell's right arm and extended it. Squatting, the guard flipped Tyrrell over his shoulder. Tyrell landed with a thud on the soft grass.

Immediately, Tyrrell got to his feet and pulled his weapon. They were in a standoff, each man pointing his gun at the other. The guard squeezed the trigger before Tyrrell did, but the shot went high and to the right. The guard fell to the ground, dead. Tony had managed to get a shot off. Tyrrell had a newfound respect for the man that just saved his life.

They rendezvoused at their point of entrance. All five members of The Unit converged behind the first hut. Rob whispered, "We'll get the guards, you get the girls." Rob motioned for Tony to follow him.

"Something's wrong. I only see one guard," Rob whispered to Tony.

"Maybe the other guy is in a hut?"

"We have to be extra careful. We still don't have Ortiz. Let's get this one, then we will search the huts."

Rob approached the man stealthily from behind. Much like he did with his first silent kill, he grabbed the man's head and snapped with a quick jerking motion and broke the man's neck. He laid him upon the grass.

Steve had moved to the mansion to find Ortiz. As he was approaching the mansion, an unaccounted for armed guard exited. The men stood frozen in that moment, too close to do anything else but throw a punch. Steve went for his gun, but the guy kicked it from his hand. Hand-to-hand combat ensued. The armed guard landed several punches to Steve's face, causing Steve to shake off the loss of consciousness he felt coming. But Steve was better than this man. He had more training. Steve bent down and went for the man's legs. He folded his body upon itself and took the man to the ground. Steve struggled to grab his knife from his boot strap. The armed guard managed to get on top of Steve. Steve knew it was now or never. The man would beat him to a pulp and then shoot him. The man began pummeling Steve's head with blows. Steve hung on just long enough to grab his knife.

Bringing his knife up, he stabbed the man in the kidney. The man hunched over and started to scream. Before any more sound could exit his mouth, Steve had his hand over the man's mouth, muffling the scream. Steve rolled him over and sliced his throat from ear to ear. Sputtering on his own blood, the man gurgled. Tiny drops shot up and hit Steve in the face. He waited until the man took his last breath before he dragged his body to the other side of the steps to be hidden by the shadows.

Rob, Tony, and Tyrrell searched the first hut. Four girls with wide, innocent eyes stared in horror. Tony spoke. "We're here to rescue you. Don't be afraid. Just wait here, and we will be back. We have to search the rest of the huts." In the second hut they reassured five girls, and in the third hut, they reassured five more. Rob couldn't help but wonder where the fuck Lola was being held. They had one more hut. The guard had to be in that hut. Lola had to be in that hut. Without thinking, Rob drew his gun and rushed the door to the last hut. He registered it all in slow motion. He saw the guard pull his gun and point it at the back of Lola's head. Without hesitation, Rob fired, killing the guard. Before he had a chance to see Lola, he heard the bang of a gun and fell to the ground. Then his world faded to black.

STRONGER

CHAPTER TWENTY-SEVEN

Rob opened his eyes to the view from his back deck. He sat there in the patio chair with a cold beer in his hand. He gazed out over the railing into the yard and admired the forest behind his house. He could hear the crickets rubbing their legs together and locusts humming. It was the dead of summer, and the sun was beginning its descent into the trees. It was a giant ball of orange flame that started to settle into the forest, darkening the sky to a dusk hour. He heard his sliding glass door open and turned his head to see his Lizzie walking through it with a glass of white wine in her hand. His mouth dropped open. He was speechless. Could he really be here with his Lizzie? It was like the last year and a half had never happened. It was just how he remembered spending summer nights with Lizzie, after they had grilled their dinner and ate on the back deck. She sat in the chair to his left and placed her wine glass on the table which separated them. He couldn't help but stare. Was he dreaming?

"Lizzie," his voice broke.

"Rob," she whispered. She had missed him. He sprang to his feet and walked quickly around the table. He lowered himself at her feet. Cradling her head in his hands, he brought her mouth to his for a possessive kiss. He kissed her as a tear slipped down his face. She was crying, too. The last time he had seen her, he was nestling her dead, limp body to his.

He broke the kiss. "How can this be?" he questioned. She would surely have the answers. She was dead. How was it he was now seeing her, kissing her as if she was alive?

"You are here with me. You can stay with me if you choose."

"What do you mean, if I choose?"

"You know, I have been watching you. I know how you feel for Lola."

Her words shocked him. "The last thing I ever wanted to do was hurt you," he confessed. "I haven't moved on yet. You have to know that. I still grieve you every day," he begged her to believe him.

"Being here has allowed me to watch you and know your heart. I know how painful my death has been to you. I have suffered here, unable to move on, because you keep me here."

"Do you want to move on, Lizzie?"

"We both have to. You have to make a choice. You can come with me and we can move on together, or you can live your life. A life I have always wanted for you. A life with Lola," Lizzie offered.

Could it be true? Could he go with her right here, right now? But what would that do to Lola?

"Since you found Lola, you have found a reason to live."

"What do you want, Lizzie? What do you want me to do? Tell me and I will do it. I will give Lola up to be with you, you know I would."

"I know. But that is not what I want for you. I want you to stay with her. I want you to live a full life and experience everything we always dreamed of experiencing."

"But don't you see. That's the problem. They were *our* dreams. How can I share our dreams with another?" Rob sobbed.

"You can raise a family with her."

"You know how I'm scared shitless at the thought of being responsible for someone so small. What if someone took my child in exchange for ransom like they did with you? I would die. And God forbid anyone hurt my child, I would never see him or her again because I would be in jail or dead," Rob emphasized.

"But you want one."

"You know I could never give you an answer one way or the other," he confessed as he choked back the sob that was threatening.

"You love Lola. I can feel it, Rob. You love me, too. But you have to let me go. You have to see what can become of you and Lola. I don't want you to give up living just to be with me."

"You don't want to be with me?" he questioned.

"That's not it. You know I will always love you. From now until eternity. But with love comes sacrifice. I would rather you live," she whispered, holding his face between her palms.

He leaned in and kissed her again. He savored the feel of her lips on his. He savored her taste. He savored her labored breathing upon his face.

"So where are we?" he asked.

"We are in between. We are where I have been since I died. You won't let me go, so I am forced to stay here. When you let me go, when you move on, you will set me free."

"Do you want me to let you go?"

"I know you will always love me. I know because I know your heart. But what you have with Lola is special and different. Not better or worse, just different. You need to be with her. You need to let me go. You need to live," she reassured him with a gentle kiss to his forehead.

"But how do I do it? I have never been able to figure out how to let you go."

"We say goodbye. Right here and right now."

"I'm not ready. Can't we at least stay and have this drink together like old times."

"Will you choose life?" she asked, still uncertain of his answer.

"I need to think about it. Will you stay with me while I think about it?" he begged of her.

"There is no place I would rather be." She smiled and it was his undoing. He bent his head forward and rested it in her lap. She gently stroked his hair while she reassured him it would be okay. She kissed the back of his head. He raised it and brought his tear stained face to her lips again. He could never get enough of his Lizzie.

"We have until the sun sets. Then you must make your decision," she informed him.

He stood up and resumed his position in the patio chair opposite her. He picked up his Coors Light and tilted it towards his lips. He gulped down a swallow. Silent, thoughtful tears continued to run down his face. Could he say goodbye to Lizzie and mean it? Could he really have a life with a woman as good as Lola? He knew he didn't deserve either woman. Still he had a choice to make. He could chose to die and spend eternity with Lizzie, or he could chose life and see what he could build with Lola. He did want to continue his work, albeit dangerous. It was the only thing he knew. He didn't know how Lola felt about that. He would never know if he chose Lizzie. Lola saved him. He owed her everything. What would it do to her if he died?

"I know your heart," Lizzie said, breaking the silence. "I want what you want."

"You know Lola saved me?"

"Yes. I know that you want to be with her, and I'm okay with that. It's time to let me go. You can't have us both. And since I'm dead," she said smiling, "I think we know what your choice must be."

"You really want me to let you go?" He just couldn't believe she would ever want him to let her go. They had a deep love. She was to be his wife.

"I want you to let me go for two reasons. One, so you can stop tormenting yourself. So you no longer feel the guilt over my death."

"I will always feel guilt over not being able to save you. That will never go away."

"Yes, but in time, and with Lola's help, you will learn to forgive yourself."

"And the second reason?"

"I want to move on. I'm tired of being stuck here. Where I am going, I will still be able to watch over you, like a guardian angel. I heard it's beautiful on the other side, and I can't wait to see it."

Rob gazed at the horizon as the dark closed in around him. "So this is really it? We are saying goodbye."

"I think it's long overdue," she said with a reassuring smile. They stood and walked to meet each other in the middle of the table. She wrapped her arms around his neck, and he wrapped his arms around her waist, pulling her closer to him until he could feel her pressed up against him.

"This is the last time I am going to feel you. The last time I am going to kiss you. You're right. I have to live. I can't give up, not even for you."

"I knew you would see it my way," she bantered, a reassuring smile playing on her lips.

He looked her directly in the eyes as his glistened with unshed tears. "Goodbye, Lizzie." He exhaled, swallowing the lump that rose in this throat.

"Goodbye, Rob. I love you. Go. Live and let yourself be loved. Do it for me," she said, smiling up at him. He brought his lips to hers for a final, goodbye kiss. He kissed her with his entire being. He felt goose bumps line his arms. This was it; this was his last kiss with Lizzie, and he was damn lucky to be getting it. He opened his mouth and begged permission to enter hers with his tongue. She granted him permission and they kissed, open-mouth, passionately until the sun finally set and the porch light no longer shone.

STRONGER

Lola had Rob's hand in hers, waiting for any sign of movement. She had her forehead rested against their joined hands as she sat by his bedside in the uncomfortable chair. He had to wake up. He had to.

Lola recounted the moments in the hut in her mind. Those moments were the worst of her life. When she was in the hut, she heard the click of the gun. She thought she was dead, but she felt nothing. She heard a louder gunshot, one that pierced her ears. She turned at the sound and saw Rob fall to the ground. Tony was in the hut the second Rob hit the ground, and he shot that bastard Ortiz right in the head. She heard his round body hit the floor. She saw the blood flow from his head and mingle with the dirt on the floor. Then her shocked gaze turned to Rob. Rob laid there, unmoving, blood pooling from his head. The smell of so much blood had turned her stomach. The sight of the man she loved, her warrior, dead on the ground was too much.

Tony didn't have to shoot the doctor as he was on his knees surrendering to Tony. She heard Tony speak into his radio.

"Rob's down." That was all he said as he approached her trembling body.

She was in shock. "What's going on?" she asked, confused.

"Rob's been shot, and you're in shock, sweetheart," Tony said with the utmost care.

She felt lightheaded, like she was going to faint. She couldn't pass out now; she had to get to Rob.

Tony knew he had to get care for Lola and for Rob. He went to Rob and she scrambled, on her knees, to kneel beside him.

She cradled Rob in her arms and said, "No. No. No," over and over again as the tears streamed down her face. She was having his baby. He couldn't die now.

Within two minutes, the rest of the team was in the hut, and Tony was dragging her from Rob's lifeless body. Other than Rob, Tyrrell was the only one with medical training. Tyrrell examined Rob and determined the bullet grazed his head. When they lifted Rob to carry him back to the RV, they noticed he had fallen on a large piece of rock, which laid flat with the compact dirt floor. They deduced he must have hit his head on the rock and knocked himself unconscious.

A day and a half later, they were back in Lewiston, and Rob was still unconscious. The doctor entered the room to examine Rob. He lifted his eyelids and shone a pen light into his eyes, looking for dilation. When his eyes didn't dilate, he looked at Lola, who was now sitting at full attention.

"What is it?" Lola whispered to the doctor.

"The CT scan we did yesterday shows a subdural hematoma. There is swelling of the subdural tissue, which is currently pressing on his brain. He will probably be unconscious until the swelling subsides."

"How long will that take?" she asked breathlessly. He had to wake up soon; they had a lot to talk about.

"He could wake up in a week or in an hour. The CT scan showed rather severe swelling," he said in his most comforting voice.

Great, no definitive answers, she thought. She hadn't called her father or her friends. The second they disembarked the airplane, she was with the men as they rushed Rob to Lewistown General Hospital. They arrived yesterday and, for most of the day, they conducted test after test on Rob. When they finally determined the cause of his state, they admitted him to the room. Lola had lied and said she was his fiancée so she would be able to stay with him. She had promised him she would be there for him, and she had meant it.

Yesterday and today gave her a great deal of time to think. Rob had saved her life, twice. Once from the unknown of being sold into slavery and a second time from being killed. He didn't know it, but he had also saved the life of their unborn child.

She needed to see a doctor. After Rob woke up, she would make an appointment. She wanted him there every step of the way with her. She didn't know if he wanted children. Having a child would mean he would have to change his lifestyle. She didn't know if she could be with someone who put his life on the line all the time, but that was who he was, and if that is what he wanted for himself, she had to trust he would always come back to her. If she was honest with herself, the dangerous aspect of his job was a major turn on for her. But the more she felt for Rob, the harder his job was to accept. What would Rob say?

If only he would wake up. Before she told him she was pregnant, she had to talk to him about what 'being his' meant. She had to tell him she would never live under any man's thumb. Ever again. Not like she did growing up under her father's roof. She would have her freedom, and if they couldn't agree on that, then she would have to say goodbye to him and raise their baby on her own. She wouldn't let this child be used to control her. She didn't think Rob meant to keep her under his thumb, but she had to make sure.

The worst part of all of this was before she found out she was pregnant, she was falling in love with Rob; knowing she was having his baby cemented her love, cemented her to him.

Rob heard people talking as if they were in another room. He heard whispers but couldn't make out the words. The last thing he remembered was kissing Lizzie goodbye. He blinked once, but the light hurts his eyes and his head throbbed. Where was he? He wasn't with Lizzie anymore. He had said his goodbye. He blinked again. "Lola," he spoke through a dry mouth and throat. It sounded more like a croak than a word.

"I'm here, baby. Open your eyes."

"Lola," he said again, feeling her squeezing his hand. He blinked in rapid succession, slowly bringing himself back into consciousness.

"Oh thank God," Lola whispered as she flung herself into his arms. He raised his arms and hugged her. "I was so scared. I thought I lost you," she cried into his chest. "I heard the gun shot and thought for sure you were gone."

"What happened?" Rob asked, confused. He could still see his goodbye with Lizzie so clearly in his mind.

"You saved my life. Again. Then Ortiz shot you and you fell and hit your head on a rock. It knocked you unconscious. You have swelling in your brain."

"How long have I been out?" he asked, even more confused.

"Three days. It took us a day to get you here. You're at Lewistown General."

He thought back and the cloud from his mind began to dissipate. He tried to sit up forcefully. "Ortiz, he was going to kill you. There was a man with a gun pointed at your head." She pushed him back down to a lying position.

"You mustn't get up until the doctor says it's okay," she warned. He pulled her to him and held her tighter. "Yes, but you killed him and then Ortiz shot you," Lola explained, trying to ease his confusion.

"How did you escape Ortiz?"

"Tony. He was in the room the second your body hit the ground." Rob looked around the room for the brother who saved his life and the life of the woman who gave his back to him, but he was nowhere to be seen.

"Where is Tony?" Rob asked.

"He's waiting in the waiting room. They won't let anyone but family back until you're awake."

"Then how are you here?" he asked, a smile playing on his lips. He knew she would have fabricated some story to stay by his side; he just knew it.

"I told them I was your fiancée," she said, hanging her head in shame.

He reached under her chin and brought her eyes up to meet his. "Well, I am glad you were the first thing I saw when I woke up," he said, placing a gentle kiss against her lips. "Can I have some water?"

"Of course." She hurried to fill the plastic cup with some water and handed it to him. The cold liquid felt so good going over his dry mouth and down his parched throat.

"We have a lot to talk about, but I don't want to rush you," Lola announced to Rob.

"I know." Rob had to tell her about his experience with Lizzie. He had to tell her he was officially all hers. But most importantly, after seeing her with a gun held to her head, he had to tell her he was in love with her. Life was too short to wait.

Just then, the doctor entered the room. "So, you're awake." The doctor smiled. Lola smiled back with great relief in her eyes. "Lola, if you would excuse us? I need to examine him," said the doctor.

"Sure, I will go tell the others you're awake. I'll be back as soon as they'll let me." She leaned in and kissed him hard, lingering at his lips. Thankful was not a strong enough word for the emotion she felt.

STRONGER

Rob was released from the hospital two days later with a bandage around his head where the bullet had grazed. He was a damn lucky man. They made their way back to Blackrain's office and headed upstairs to Tyrrell's office for a debriefing. Each member of the team gave their report and answered an hour's worth of questions. Tyrrell needed to justify the expenditures to Mr. Sardeson. He needed complete reports and guarantees that all parties who were a danger to Lola were now neutralized. Of course, Tyrrell knew this, he was there. But a full report was what he needed. When Rob was done with his portion, he walked into the hall.

Rob found Lola in the hallway leaning up against the wall. "Come on, I'll show you where you will be staying while you're here." Rob extended his hand, and Lola placed her delicate hand into Rob's larger one. He intertwined their fingers and led her down the hallway to one of the bedrooms. Tyrell had rooms made into bedrooms because teammates frequently needed to stay overnight to ready for a mission. Rob picked the room at the far end of the hall and opened the door. The room had cream colored walls and a bed against the far wall. The bed was made with a maroon colored comforter, and to Lola's surprise, the curtains matched the bedspread. Someone had good taste.

"Sorry there is no dresser. You will have to live out of your suitcase for a while."

"What about you?" Lola questioned as she looked at him with fear in her eyes. "We have so much to talk about."

He leaned in and pressed his soft, formable lips to hers. He kissed her with an appreciation she had never known. When he broke the kiss, the right side of his lips curled up until he was grinning.

"I'll never grow tired of your kisses," Rob assured her.

"Rob, we have to talk," Lola cajoled, turning away from him. She needed to know where she stood so she could get her baby the care he or she needed.

"I know Lizzie will always hold a place in your heart, and I don't want to take that away from her or you. But you have to let her go if you want to move on with me." She turned back around to face him. To her surprise, he stood there, smiling a goofy grin. "What could you possibly be smiling about? I know how you feel about her," Lola debated.

"I wanted to talk to you about Lizzie and what happened between us."

"I don't understand. What do you mean? What happened?"

"Let me explain. Here, sit down," he said, extending his arm to her back and leading her to the bed. She sat down and looked up at him with wide eyes.

"Something happened while I was unconscious, and you are going to think I am crazy, but I swear to you, it really happened."

"Okay, what," she drawled out.

"I saw Lizzie in a place she called the in between. She gave me a choice. I could go with her, or I could come back to you."

Tears instantly formed in Lola's eyes. She saw the peace in Rob's eyes when he spoke of his encounter with Lizzie.

"There's more."

"Go on," she said, wiping the tears from her face with the back of her hand.

"I kissed her…goodbye."

"Does that mean you're all mine?" Lola asked, a smile threatening her lips.

"I will make you a deal. I will be all yours, if you are all mine," he said, playing with her.

"Before I can answer that, we have to talk about something pretty important to me," Lola responded. Rob looked at her with both eyes. She was serious. He had never seen her so serious before. Whatever it was, it was greatly important to her. He would do his best to reassure her. He couldn't lose her now that he had finally found the woman he could love for all eternity.

What was it about Rob that possessed her soul so completely? He was domineering, and she didn't want to live under anyone's thumb. Sure, he was incredibly gorgeous. He was tall, muscular, had the perfect specimen of a body. He had an eight-pack of rock hard abs. She took care of herself physically, so she wanted someone who cared about his body in the same way.

But it was more than his looks. It was the way he cared for her. She always wanted a man to take care of her emotionally. She knew Rob was not a weak man, and yet he had shown his vulnerability to her. Was it how he placed her above all else? Wasn't that what love was? Did he love her? He wanted her to say she was his. He was finally over Lizzie, one hurdle down, two more to go. She definitely wanted a future with him, or she would never have given herself to him. Was Rob her forever? She thought about it as she stared down at her feet and chose her words.

She gathered her strength and courage for the conversation to come, because she knew he could squash all of her hopes and dreams of a future with him if he couldn't get his caveman tendencies under control when it came to her.

She lifted her eyes to his and stared for a moment, amassing her scattering courage. She didn't want to lose him. Ever. She patted the spot beside her on the bed. "Here, sit down with me." He sat down beside her. She tucked her legs under her body and sat so she was facing him. He mimicked her pose.

"What is it, love? You're scaring me," Rob confessed.

"I need to talk to you about what you said about wanting to 'own' me. I thought that was pillow talk, but you said it again."

Rob stood up and began pacing. He knew this was too good to be true. He ran his hand roughly over his face and through his hair. Then he stopped short in front of her and got on his knees. He took her hands in both of his and looked up at her through his dark, thick lashes with both eyes.

"Please don't say it. I know I got carried away. It was just seeing you there, in front of me, it brought feelings I didn't know I was feeling to the surface. I am so sorry if I scared you. I just need you to know I would die for you. Shit, I have killed to protect you, and I would do it again, in a heartbeat. I would never do anything to hurt you."

"God. No. Rob, it isn't about that. I know you would never hurt me. But it is about what you meant when you asked me to be yours. I'm just going to say it. I'm going to lay my cards on the table and let the pieces fall where they may."

Rob bowed his head.

"Look at me, Rob." She broke free from his hands and took his face in her hands. She tilted his face up until their eyes met. "You've got me. I'm not going anywhere."

Rob's shoulders slumped and he exhaled. He had been holding his breath, so afraid she was going to end it. "So what is it? What do you want to ask me?" Rob questioned, much calmer than he was a few minutes ago.

"What will it mean to be yours? Because I won't live under anyone's thumb ever again. You don't get to control what I do or who my friends are. You don't get to tell me where I'm allowed to go and when I'm allowed to go out. Those are my choices, and if being yours involves any of that, then I can't do it. I am so sorry, because I want to do it, but I can't. Not after everything I have been through with Daddy."

"Love, no. I would never mean to control you like that. Being mine means just that. You're mine and no one else's. I don't mean to control your behavior. Well, maybe inside the bedroom." He waggled his brow at her. She smiled. "Being mine means just that you belong to me and no one else. You and I are exclusive. We have a relationship. I don't want you to be anyone other than who you are. You can pick your own friends; I just hope they like me."

A tear fell from her eye and ran down her cheek. That was the answer she had been praying for. She wanted to be with Rob in the worst way, but not at the expense of herself.

"What are the tears for? Did I say something wrong?"

"No. God no. You said everything right." She leaned down and pressed her firm lips against his soft ones. She kissed him with everything she had. They could make this work. She flicked her tongue over his bottom lip before sucking it into her mouth. She brushed her lips over his in a sweet gesture meant to comfort and encourage him.

He kissed her with a passion that was unknown to him. He had never felt anything like it before. He would die for the woman in his arms.

Just then there was a knock at the door. Rob broke the kiss and swore under his breath. "Rob, you can't leave yet. There is something else rather important I need to tell you."

Holding Lola was the only place he wanted to be. "Let me see who it is." He strode to the door and opened it.

"Sorry. Did I interrupt something?" Tony asked with a grin a mile wide on his face. He knew damn well he interrupted something. "Boss wants us. He's talked to the FBI."

Rob looked back at Lola before leaving the room. He followed Tony down the hall to Tyrrell's office. "Come in. Sit down," Tyrrell ordered. Tony and Rob entered the office and each sat in a leather-backed chair placed in front of Tyrrell's desk.

"My contacts at the FBI have confirmed that the Ortiz Cartel is officially wiped off the face of the earth. Ortiz never had any sons, so no one will be coming to seek revenge against Lola. She's free to go home."

STRONGER

Rob came back to the room to find Lola lying down on the bed. He couldn't blame her after the ordeal she had been through. He wanted to let her sleep, but she looked too delicious. The sun had set hours ago, and they had the office to themselves. Everyone else had left for the evening. She was his. All his. To do with as he pleased. He approached the bed and nuzzled her neck, bringing her out of a deep sleep. She blinked her eyes open at him. "You haven't eaten yet, and I insist you do. I don't want you getting sick."

He was right, she had to eat for the baby. She still needed to tell him, but it could wait until morning. They should have tonight to celebrate their love.

"I will be downstairs in the kitchen. Get some clothes on and come join me. I'll whip us up something quick."

Lola got dressed in a pair of cut-off shorts and a tank top. She walked downstairs and found Rob in the kitchen gathering the ingredients to cook for her. She wouldn't allow it. She wanted to prove to Rob that she wasn't a spoiled princess. She wanted to prove that she was a woman that knew how to care for a man—a man like Rob. She reached for the carton of eggs and took them from Rob.

"You know, my breakfast staples are for when the girls and I go out on the weekends. We go back to my place and hang out. They sleep on the couch and in the spare rooms. Then we get up in the morning and have eggs, bacon, toast, and orange juice. Sound good?"

"Sounds perfect. Thank you."

Lola turned from Rob and started cracking eggs into a bowl. Rob approached her from behind. He placed his hands on her thighs, startling her because he was so quiet. He slid them up under her shirt, under her bra, to her breasts. As he palmed them, she laid her head back against his chest. She enjoyed the feeling of him pressed against her back. He brought his mouth to her neck, and she could feel his hot breath upon her. He nipped at her flesh and then soothed the bite with a kiss. He continued nipping his way up her neck to her earlobe. Once there, he stopped and suckled it into his mouth and bit down hard. Lola moaned her acceptance of the pain and placed her hand behind her on his thigh. She ran her hand up as far as she could but couldn't reach his cock. He suckled her earlobe as he rolled her nipples between his thumbs and forefingers, pinching them slightly before letting them go. He ran his hands slowly down her body and lifted her shirt.

"Take off your shorts," Rob commanded. She complied, and God have mercy, she was wearing a lacy pair of thong panties.

"Turn around," he demanded. She did as she was told and turned in the caged space. He was pressed up against her front. He grabbed her by the waist and lifted her onto the counter.

"What are you doing?" she asked coyly, looking up at him through her long, dark lashes. "Aren't there people here?" she questioned.

"It's just us. Everyone else has left for the night."

He brought his hot mouth over hers in a demanding and rough kiss. Their teeth scraped and he thrust his firm tongue into her mouth. Like before, she sucked on it and was rewarded by his moan.

His hand followed her arm down her side and found her moist center. "God, you're wet," he said as he ran his finger up and down her clit through the lace of her panties. He traced the edge of her panties, teasing her with things to come all while kissing her possessively. He scooted her panties to the side and thrust a finger inside her body. She moaned into his mouth. His finger felt so good, but she was hungry for something more, something bigger.

"I want your cock, Rob," she said forcefully through gritted teeth. Location be damned. They could watch their fill. She wanted him. A fever ignited inside her and could only be controlled with Rob's cock buried deep within her.

She reached in front of her and fumbled at the button on his jeans. Figures, button fly. She fumbled with each button, but eventually got his pants down past his ass. He helped her slide his pants to his knees. Then he slid her panties to the side and pressed his cock to her entrance.

"I am going to fuck you hard, okay?" he told her as he reached into his wallet and pulled out a condom. He had himself sheathed with it before she had a chance to protest that he no longer needed it. She wasn't ready to have that conversation. She wanted to enjoy him. She responded by nodding her head and biting her bottom lip.

He lost it at the sight of her bottom lip between her teeth. The way she was looking at him said she could eat him alive and spit out the bones. He met her eyes and saw the same passion, the same desire, the same possession he felt. He thrust hard inside her in one move. God she was so tight. He stilled because he didn't want to hurt her.

"What are you waiting for? Fuck me," Lola demanded.

Rob wrapped her hair around his hand and placed his hand under her ass cheek to angle her so he could penetrate deeper. He thrust inside her harder and faster. With each thrust he pulled her hair until she screamed. He wanted to make her scream with the same desire he knew. Faster and deeper he thrust until his balls were bouncing off her ass. Her legs were wrapped firmly around his thighs. She matched his rhythm with counter thrusts of her own. Her head was pulled the whole way back, which gave Rob unobscured access to her neck. He bit her, then licked at the wound. He did it again, and she screamed his name.

He had her bound by her hair, unable to move her head as he thrust into her over and over again. With each thrust she approached the edge. He bit her again and pain shot through her body, but his thrusting quickly turned the bite mark into pleasure. She wanted desperately to bite him back. To be rough with him. She reached around him and used her nails to dig her way down his back. She was sure she drew blood with how hard she dug her nails in. It was the most exquisite kind of pain. Pain that caused his momentum to increase. She was so close.

"I'm going to come all over your cock while it's buried deep inside my pussy," she said. She found it turned her on to say dirty things to him while he fucked her. It was one of the ways she had of controlling him.

With her words, Rob's body tensed. "Come with me, love," he said, loosening his hold on her hair. "Look into my eyes and come with me." He exhaled as his body went rigid and his hot seed filled her while her hot, tight pussy convulsed around his thick, hard cock. Their eyes met as they lost themselves to this world. He continued spurting his seed into her with slow, deep thrusts, while her pussy continued to suck him dry.

They stayed in each other's embrace, staring into each other's eyes communicating words left unspoken between them. She blinked as she started to come down from her orgasm-induced high. His body started to relax and she could feel his cock going semi-soft inside her.

"Good thing we're alone," she said as a smile touched her lips.

When Rob had started to touch her, she had forgotten everything but him. The way he claimed her, marked her, controlled her was the most inviting thing she had ever experienced. She was lost to this man. This domineering, tough, muscular, down-to-earth man. Just thinking about how he possessed her made her want more of him. She pressed her thighs together, trying to dull the ache that was constant when she thought of Rob, when she was near Rob. She reached up and kissed his lips in a possessive kiss demanding he kiss back.

"Thank you," she said when she pulled back.

"For what?"

"Rescuing me, protecting me, wanting me."

"Love, you don't have to ever thank me for that. I should be thanking you." He leaned in and covered her lips with his hot mouth, kissing her reverently. He brushed his lips lightly over hers before he devoured her in a soul-aching kiss.

CHAPTER
THIRTY-ONE

Rob's eyes squinted against the afternoon sun that shone directly into the room through the sheers, which were hanging over the bedroom windows. He looked to Lola lying there so peaceful; he didn't have the heart to wake her up. What he saw took his breath away. She lay on her side, arm tucked under her pillow, blonde hair fanning down her side and onto the mattress. He ran his rough hand up and down her exposed skin, marveling at the soft feel. When he completed two passes of her arm, she opened her eyes and smiled suggestively at him.

"Good morning," she cooed.

"Good morning. Come here," he demanded as he moved his body closer to hers. She turned fully on her side and moved into him. Her body was now pressed firmly up against his. He lifted his leg and her leg fell in between his. He tightened his grip around her so that not as much as a molecule of air existed between them. He brushed his lips over hers in a teasing manner. She caught his bottom lip and suckled it into her hot mouth. He moaned a guttural sound from deep within his body and pressed his pelvis into hers. She responded by pressing against his erection with her body. He ran his hand through her hair, over and over as he kissed her gently and thoroughly. He used his tongue to part her lips, begging for entrance into her mouth. She obliged, and he thrust his tongue into her mouth while he grabbed and wrapped her hair around his hand. He turned her head to accept the angle of his mouth as he intensified the kiss. He moved his free hand, which lay under his head, to caress her face. He stroked her cheek gently as he pulled her hair roughly.

The contrasting signals her body was receiving sent Lola into a spin. She loved to be kissed gently while having her hair pulled. It was the perfect combination in her opinion.

He nudged her over so he could press his erection against her backside. He pressed a tender kiss to her spine and continued with tender kisses up her back until he reached her neck. He moved her hair to the side of her body and pressed firm lips against the center of her neck. She began to moan and move her hips back into his, gyrating against his hard cock.

This morning, she was going to ask him to show her what he liked. She rolled over again to face him, and he groaned at the loss of the feel of her ass pressed firmly against his member.

"I have a surprise for you," she said, playfully smiling down at him as she got to a kneeling position.

"Oh yeah, what's that?"

She pushed his shoulder back to touch the bed so that he was now lying on his back. She crawled and then straddled his pelvic area.

"I'm not wearing any underwear," she said playfully as she rubbed herself unashamedly up and down the length of his hard cock.

"Let me join you." He smiled up at her.

She removed her leg from his side and went back into the kneeling position.

"I like the way you look when you kneel like that. Like you're waiting for me to do naughty things to you," Rob assessed.

"This morning I'm going to do naughty things to you. I want you to show me how. You're my first, so I have never been on top. But I want to. I want to fuck you today," she confessed with a sultry look in her eyes. She moved so she was straddling him again. She felt his large cock nestled in between her folds and pressed right up against her clit. She bent forward and kissed the long scar that ran from the top of his chest across one pectoral muscle while she slid back and forth against his rock hard erection.

"You're going to kill me," Rob confessed as he placed his hands on her hips. He lifted slightly and his cock sprang up and met the entrance to her pussy. She pushed her hips down slowly, and they both moaned at the feel of his thick cock entering her tight pussy.

"Show me how," she demanded.

"Just do whatever feels good to you. I promise if you do that, it will feel twice as good to me."

She began rocking back and forth against him. She lifted and seated herself again and again on his cock. But the friction was what felt really good to her. So she placed her hands behind her on his thighs and started moving against him so that she bumped her clit into his pelvic bone with each thrust. Rob couldn't take it anymore. He had to be closer to her. He had to touch more than her hips. He sat up, and she wrapped her arms around his neck. Her large breasts molded to his muscular chest. She placed her legs in front of her so she was now seated on him. She used her feet to push back and forth against him as he thrust himself into her. Push and pull, thrust and bump, she was nearing the edge.

"This is supposed to be about you. I'm going to come if you keep up this rhythm," she moaned.

"I am right there with you. Just hold on with me, love. We come together today."

He pressed his lips firmly against her mouth. She opened her lips, allowing his tongue access. She was lost in the kiss. All she could do was hold on and let him kiss her. She kept her mouth open. "Yes," she cried.

"Yes," he returned.

"Yes," she cried again. She felt his body tense.

"Come now," he demanded.

His words were her undoing. She shattered, stars appearing behind her closed eyes. She had ahold of his hair and was pulling it hard when she started to come back into herself. They stayed entwined in each other's arms for several minutes, making love with their mouths. They kissed and nipped. Nipped and licked at each other, trying to express what each one meant to the other. Rob felt it so very deeply he could never erase her. She was it for him. These thoughts played on his mind as he tightened his hold around her body.

She didn't mind it. She loved being held, caressed, dominated, anything by this man.

She slowly rose from his body, his semi-hard cock falling from the holds of her perfect, tight pussy. "Let's get a shower and clean you up," he said, pressing his soft lips against the tip of her nose.

In the bathroom he removed her t-shirt.

"What about breakfast? Aren't you hungry?" she asked him.

"After our shower. I need to take care of you first," he pointed out as he turned on the shower faucets to find the perfect temperature. "Do you like your showers warm or hot?"

"Hot," she replied. He tested the temperature to make sure it wasn't too hot and then held open the door for her to enter. He stepped in after her. He grabbed a body buff and squeezed some shower gel onto it. He lathered it up and started to cleanse her body. He took his time washing every inch of her flesh. When he was done, he rinsed her with the removable shower head.

Once she was rinsed, he tilted her head back and wet her hair. Then he squeezed some shampoo into his hands and massaged it into her scalp. She moaned in delight. No one had bathed her since she was a little girl. *She could get used to this.* When he was done with his lavish massage of her scalp, he applied the conditioner and massaged that in, too. He rinsed her hair.

She had to take equal care of him, so she reached for the body buff, but he wouldn't let her. He made quick work of washing himself and his hair while she traced his back muscles with her fingertips. Her touch was undoing him and his erection was straining, pointing upwards towards his navel. When he turned in her arms, she felt him hard against her. Although she was sore, she didn't want to disappoint Rob, so she got to her knees. She lovingly looked up at Rob from her position on the floor of the shower as she grabbed his cock firmly in her hand. She rubbed the tip of his cock against her lips while maintaining eye contact.

Rob lost control of himself. "You are so goddamned sexy. I will kill anyone who tries to take you from me. You are mine. Do you hear me? All mine. God, you're fucking unbelievable. You belong to me! Say that you are mine," he rambled to her through gritted teeth. She sparked a fire that raged in him. He had to hear her say it again, but she remained tight lipped. She couldn't say it again until she told him about her pregnancy.

She couldn't speak because she chose that moment to place his cock inside her hot mouth. She drew her lips tight around his large cock. She used her hand to stroke his length while she sucked as much as she could into her mouth. He was huge. There was no way she could fit all of him inside her mouth. She stroked him with a tight fist. She withdrew him from her mouth and spit on the head of his cock. He stared intently at the sight. She used her hand to move the saliva up and down the length of him as she sucked him back inside, flicking the tip of his head with her tongue. He reached down and tilted her head up so she could look at him. The sight of her with his cock in her mouth made him go caveman on her.

"Say it now. Say that you are mine. I swear to God I will kill anyone that tries to take you from me. I will protect you always, but you have to tell me. Tell me you are mine. I have to hear it from your lips again." She opened her throat and took him deeper still. She kept her throat open as she fisted his length, bringing his cock in and out of her mouth in rhythm with her hand. She sucked hard. She reached her free hand around and started to spread his ass cheeks. He let her. She pushed a finger at the opening of his anus as she sucked harder. She wiggled her finger back and forth, pressing it into him.

"Fuck! Do you have any idea what you are doing to me? Fuck," he growled.

She pushed in a little further with her finger, opened her throat, wrapped her full lips firmly around his head, flicked his head with her tongue, and then sucked him into her throat. She felt his body tense.

"I'm going to come."

She continued to stroke his length while she sucked and fucked his cock with her mouth. He started to tremble and she knew she had him. She felt the hot seed hit her tongue and she swallowed around his cock. The swallowing created a vacuum for him. "Fuck me," he yelled as he finished shooting his seed into her mouth and she finished by swallowing it all. Every last drop. He was still trembling. His legs were shaking.

She stood up and looked him straight in the eye. "What was your question?" Oh, how she loved to tease.

"God damn it, Lola. Tell me you are mine. I am going out of my mind here."

She remained silent. She had to tell him about the baby first. If he couldn't accept the baby, then she couldn't be his.

CHAPTER
THIRTY-TWO

Down in the kitchen they grabbed a cereal bar and a banana for lunch. Rob even made a turkey sandwich because sex that morning with Lola had given him an appetite.

"Is that all you're eating?" Rob asked when Lola could not finish her banana.

Lola's face flushed. She needed to find the right time to tell him about her pregnancy, and she needed somewhere private to do it.

"Would you mind coming back to the room with me? I need to talk to you," Lola asked cautiously. She had no idea how Rob felt on the issue of children, but if he wasn't on board, she was out of there. She didn't want to be with someone who didn't want kids. As much as she was falling in love with this man, it was more than her feelings at stake now. She had a baby to think about. She really prayed Rob would take the news well. She hoped this wouldn't break their fragile relationship. It was so new. They hadn't even confessed feelings to each other yet. Yes, he had said he was hers, but would that include a child? That was a big commitment to ask from him. Although he was talking like it was forever with them. He was willing to die for her, and he had proven that fact when he got shot. That had to mean he had feelings for her. But would they be enough?

"Sure." He playfully nuzzled her neck and she pulled away from him.

"This is serious, Rob. I need to have a serious talk with you."

"Sure. Lead the way." Rob followed Lola to the back bedroom they had claimed as theirs for the next day.

Lola held the door open for Rob and waited for him to enter before shutting and locking the door.

"What's wrong, love? You're scaring me again. All these serious conversations," he cooed as he playfully pulled her to him to kiss her lips. She let his lips linger and eventually gave into his passion and kissed him back.

She pressed both hands on his hard chest and pushed him back at the same time she pulled from his body. She had to have a clear head to have this conversation.

"You better sit down," she said as she motioned to the bed for him to sit.

Lola began pacing back and forth as she twisted her fingers with her hand. She caught herself and smoothed her shirt flat against her body. She cleared her throat trying to gather her courage to say what needed to be said.

She went to the door of the room, far away from the bed, to distance herself physically from his reaction, not that she thought he would physically hurt her. She brought her hand up to her lips and tugged on her bottom one. She left her hand there as she began to speak. "Look, I know we"—she gestured between the two of them with her free hand—"are new to this relationship. I know what you went through letting Lizzie go to attempt a relationship with me. And what I have to tell you could ruin it."

Rob was immediately standing and closing the distance between them. She struggled free of his hold and moved to the other side of the room. She turned to face him, her face feeling aflame.

"Now you are seriously scaring me. Tell me you aren't leaving me. Tell me we can work out the distance thing," he pleaded, hoping to calm her and bring back the Lola he knew and loved. The fearless woman who stomped on the foot of a killer and kneed him in the balls. This frightened and insecure Lola was scaring the shit out of him.

She was going to have to say it. As Rob approached her, she held out her hand to stop him. "Rob, I'm pregnant."

Stunned, he plopped himself on the bed, unable to stand. Of all the things she could have said, being pregnant wasn't on his radar. He had used protection, how was this even possible?

"But I used a condom," he croaked, rubbing his forearm with his hand.

"I don't know, Rob. It must have broke. You were my first." His words were not the words that would lead her to her dream. She would give him the benefit of the doubt and let him process. She didn't like his reaction so far.

"I'll leave you alone with your thoughts. When you're ready, come and get me." She hurried to the door. She had to get out of the room as the walls were closing in on her. He wasn't happy. If anything he looked devastated. She hurried down the hallway to the bathroom. She was going to be sick. Rob didn't want this baby. *Give him the benefit of the doubt. Let him think about it.* The thoughts plagued her mind. Raising a baby by herself. Harvard was her father's dream. She wanted a family and a husband. She wanted nothing more than to stay home and devote every waking hour to her family. Now the dreams of a family, a family with Rob, were in jeopardy. She gave herself to him, and he had given her the gift of a child. No matter what he decided, she was in love with him and probably always would be.

When she was done throwing up, she wiped her hand with the toilet paper she had gathered. She stepped to the sink to rinse her mouth, and furiously brush her teeth to remove the taste. It had become a ritual over the last two weeks. Of course, being held prisoner, she had to deal with the taste, no toothbrush. She finished and placed her toothbrush back on the sink. She reached for the doorknob and opened the door quickly to find Rob, head hung, staring at his feet as she did so.

"You ready?" she asked, sensing what his reaction was going to be. He wasn't happy, which is the only reaction she would have accepted from him.

She padded down the hallway to the bedroom and sat on the bed. Her hard part was over, now it was Rob's turn.

"You have options," he said, looking at her with dead gray eyes.

She stood and stalked to Rob. When she reached him, she struck him across his face, leaving her handprint. "The only option I am considering is keeping this baby, Rob," she spat out because she was so angry. Her eyes were hard. She tightened her eyes to look at him in disgust.

"That's all you have to say? I have options?" Her voice raised an octave. "I have to get out of here," she said, racing towards the door.

Rob stood there, hand to his face where she had slapped him. He had just let the woman he was in love with down. And worse, he just let her walk right out of his life.

Lola raced down the hallway barging into Tyrrell's office. "Can I use your phone?" she asked as sobs racked her body. She was racing away from the only man she was ever in love with. But how could she stay?

"Are you okay?" Tyrrell asked.

"No. And I need to go home now," she said, anger raging through her body.

"Sure," he said as he turned his phone around and pushed it to Lola's side of the desk. Rob hadn't even come after her. She was supposed to be his. She shook her head and dialed her father's airline for reservations to Boston.

"I need the first flight out to Boston," she said into the phone. "That will be fine." She covered the receiver with her hand and looked at Tyrrell with tear-filled eyes. "Can you give me a ride to the airport?"

"Sure. Are you sure that's what you want?"

She nodded her head as tears streamed down her face. "I'll be there. Thank you," she sobbed. She walked back to the room expecting to find Rob still there, but he was gone. Figures, when she really needed him, he disappeared. She threw her things in her bag and stomped back to Tyrrell's office. "I'm ready."

"Sure. One minute." Tyrrell grabbed his gun and tucked it into his holster before grabbing his suit coat from the back of his chair.

"Ready?" he asked her, motioning for her to lead the way.

Tyrrell followed her out of Blackrain Security and drove her to the airport.

CHAPTER
THIRTY-THREE

Rob sat in the dimly lit room. The full moon was shining through the open curtains. He stared at the moon with a bottle of scotch in his hand. Bringing his hand to his mouth, he took a swig from the bottle and felt the smooth burn as the liquid traveled down his throat.

His head was heavy and rested in his hand. He kept thinking over and over of letting Lola walk out of his life. He let her go. Why? Was he that much of a coward? She was pregnant with his child. His child. What would be like to hold his child in his arms? He never wanted one, but now it was different. He had no choice; he was going to have a child out in the big bad world that belonged to him and the love of his life. Lola. Now it was thoughts of Lola that plagued his mind. She was all he could think about. He missed her smell, her taste, her touch. He missed her bold attitude and the way she kissed him. He realized now he was deeply in love with her. But what could he do; he couldn't put a child in danger's path. And that is exactly what he would be doing by claiming his child. He had to let her go. He had to let the love of his life and his child go for their own safety.

He took another long swallow from the bottle. He placed the bottle on the table next to his chair when he heard pounding on his front door. He considering not answering it, but the pounding continued louder than before. Getting up, he ambled his way to the door. Not caring who was on the other side, he yanked the door open.

"You gonna let me in?" Michael asked.

Rob opened the door wider and moved to the side so Michael could enter his home. Rob should be embarrassed by the state of his home, but he wasn't. He didn't care about anything at the moment, except his misery over letting Lola go.

Michael strode past Rob into the living room. Eying the half-empty bottle of scotch on the table, he turned to Rob.

"I heard you were doing better?" he questioned Rob.

"I was," Rob said as he made his way back to his chair and plopped down.

"What happened? I heard you met an extraordinary woman."

"I did. I would die for her."

"Then what the fuck are you doing sitting here feeling sorry for yourself?" Michael cut to the chase.

"You don't understand, Michael. She's pregnant," Rob said, devoid of emotion.

Michael met Rob's eyes. He knew Rob was hurting. He had missed a great deal in the weeks he had been gone on his honeymoon.

"Do you love her?" Michael needed the answer to this question in order to know which direction to proceed. Michael had a good feeling he knew the answer, but getting Rob to admit it to him was half the battle.

"I am in love with her. Have been since the moment I laid eyes on her. She touched me instantly, in a way no one ever has."

Michael raised his eyebrows, and his eyes went wide at the statement. When he left, Rob was still reeling over the guilt of losing Lizzie. Whoever this woman was, Rob had to get her back. Whatever it took. She was good for his friend.

"What about Lizzie? I thought you were still in love."

Rob told Michael about what happened with Lizzie while he was unconscious in the hospital. At the end of the story, Michael stood and began to pace.

"Why did you let her go? She's carrying your child!" Michael didn't understand. When Emma became pregnant, which they were working on, he would be the happiest man alive.

"I would never admit this to anyone but you or Tony, but I'm scared shitless. What if someone uses my child against me while on a mission? What if someone hurts my child? You know I would lose my shit and start killing people. What good would I be to Lola or my child if I'm in jail or dead? What if I wasn't a good father? My father left my mother when I was an infant. You know how my mother struggled raising me," Rob confessed, feeling a little freer.

"Exactly! You want to do the same thing to your child? Leave him before he is even born?" Michael reasoned.

Rob took another long swallow from the bottle. Walking straight to Rob, Michael snatched the bottle out of his hand and went to the kitchen. He knew Rob would be pissed, but he would get over it. Pouring the contents of the bottle down the sink, he threw the empty bottle into the trashcan and found the coffee filters. He placed grounds in the basket and water in the coffee pot. He waited until a cup had brewed before pouring a strong, black cup for Rob. Michael reentered the living room with coffee in hand. "Here, you need to be sober. You need to know, without booze clouding your judgment, exactly what you are throwing away," Michael chided.

Rob took the coffee from Michael's extended hand. Making his way to the couch, Michael sat and waited for Rob to drink his coffee before continuing. Once Rob had finished, Michael suggested a cold shower to sober him up.

"I don't want to feel." Rob exhaled.

"Afraid of what you might feel? Afraid of facing the fuckwad mistake you made?" Michael wasn't holding back. Lola was good for Rob, and Michael knew it. He just had to get Rob to see it, too.

"Fine," Rob spat as he got to his feet and made his way upstairs.

Michael grabbed the remote control from the table and found the news. Placing the remote back on the table, he made his way into the kitchen and made himself a cup of coffee. It was going to be a long night.

Appearing dressed in basketball shorts and a t-shirt, Michael knew Rob was sober by the emotion he saw playing in his eyes. Michael had seen Rob at his absolute lowest after Lizzie died. He had seen Rob cry unashamedly, and he was there for him then and he would be there for him now. Michael approached his brother and extended his hand. Rob took it, and Michael pulled him into a one-arm hug. Rob took solace in Michael for a moment before pulling back.

"What the fuck am I supposed to do?" Rob asked with a broken voice. "I'm in love with her, but I'm scared shitless."

"Having a baby is scary as fuck. Emma and I are trying to conceive right now, and I know the fears you feel. But you can't let the fear hold you back. You *are* having a baby. I assume she is keeping it?"

"When I suggested options, she stormed out," Rob told his brother.

"Well then, you just have to get her back."

"You make it sound so easy. I have legitimate fears."

"Let me ask you a question. Would your life be better or worse with Lola and a baby?"

Rob sat silent for a few moments, carefully thinking of the question. In his heart, he knew Lola was the only woman for him. But how did he get over the fears of having a baby?

"During the time I was with Lola, my life was worth living. She made everything about my life okay. She even helped me work on forgiving myself for not saving Lizzie."

Looking Rob dead in the eyes, Michael asked, "Why the fuck do you think being without her would be better for you? Why the fuck don't you want the child you created out of love with this woman? You are going to have a son or daughter that is part of you. Do you really want to miss out on seeing him take his first steps? Hearing him say Dad for the first time?"

"I hadn't thought about what having a child would be like. I have only thought about the 'what ifs.'"

"Here is a 'what if' for you…what if Lola meets another man who wants to raise your child as his own?"

Rob was instantly on his feet. He clenched his fists at his side. He hadn't given that any thought.

"From what I heard from Tony, Lola is a beautiful woman. It won't take her long to find a man who won't abandon her when she needs him the most."

"What the fuck have I done?" Rob asked, hanging his head in his hands. He turned his back on Michael and swallowed down the lump forming in his throat. The gravity of the situation was weighing on him. He couldn't stand the thought of Lola with another man. But more than that, he couldn't stand the idea of another man raising his child.

Turning back to face Michael, Rob looked at him with a broken heart. "What the fuck do I do? I can't let that happen. I want her more than I'm afraid of the 'what ifs.' I want my child to know his father. I want to be a part of his life even if she won't have me back after deserting her in her time of need."

"She loves you. That's what Tony told me."

"How would Tony know?" Rob questioned. If she loved him, that would change everything.

"She hinted that she loved you to Tony. She never left your side at the hospital. She was willing to stick by your side while you found a way to let Lizzie go," Michael stated his case.

"How could you possibly know all of this?" Rob questioned his brother.

"I talked to The Unit and every one of those motherfuckers agree, she loves you, man. She may not have said it out of fear of scaring you away. You were trying to let Lizzie go, but she never left your side until you told her to go by suggesting she get rid of your child," Michael reassured his friend.

"I love her, man. How the fuck do I get her back?"

"Is she worth the fight?" Michael asked.

"Fuck yeah. She's my everything, and she is the mother of my child."

"Then you fight for her, and you don't give up. Chances are she is gonna push against you. She's gonna make you prove yourself. So you do just that. You don't let up; you don't stop; you find a way to make her listen to you. And when she does, you tell her exactly what you told me. Tell her all of your fears. If she really loves you, she will understand. I'm sure she's scared shitless, too," Michael offered.

With a new sense of purpose and clarity he never knew before, Rob stood and approached his brother, opening his arms. Michael stood and stepped into Rob's embrace. Rob hugged him tight. Michael spoke truth and sense. He didn't know where he would be without Michael and Tony. They saved his life more than a few times. They were joined at the soul level. He would die for any of them and the women they loved, and he knew they would give their lives for him and the woman he loved. They shared a brotherhood that very few people knew.

Rob released Michael and pulled back.

"I hope it's not too late," Rob declared.

"It's only been a few days. True love is hard to get over. You, better than anyone, know that."

"This thing with Lola is more than I ever experienced before. It is so different from what I experienced with Lizzie. I never felt this urgency, this need to possess so completely. I have to make her mine in all ways," Rob confessed.

"What are talking about, man? I think it is a little too early to propose."

"I don't think anything else will do. I have to ask her to marry me. I have to know she is mine forever. I have to know she will never keep my child from me. I need to be there to care for her and the child in every way possible," Rob appealed for his friend's understanding.

"Yeah, but you've only known her a few weeks. That is too soon to ask someone to marry you," Michael cautioned.

"I can ask her and then we can have a long engagement. I want my ring on her finger. I want to be everything to her, the same way she is everything to me," Rob declared more confident in his decision than ever before. If she really did love him like he loved her, he felt confident she would say yes. She was devastated when he spoke to her last. Devastation like that only exists in true love. She had given him the power to destroy her. That meant he also had the power to restore her.

Rob extended his hand to Michael. When Michael clasped his hand with Rob's, Rob covered it with his free hand. "Thank you. I can't thank you enough. I was going to let her go. I was just going to let her and my child go. Thank you for knowing me better than I know myself sometimes. I can never repay you," Rob said, squeezing Michael's hand with both of his.

STRONGER

On the airplane, Rob pulled the ring from his pocket to look at it again. It was a beautiful square cut diamond which sat slightly atop the setting. The center one-carat diamond, which he used some of his savings to purchase, was surrounded by brilliant square cut diamonds. He had picked the ring out himself. Now he just had to get her to agree to wear it.

Rob recalled telling Tony and Tyrrell he needed the company jet to fly to Boston to ask the woman of his dreams, the mother of his child, to marry him. Since there were no missions at the present time, Tyrrell agreed to lend him the jet. He knew he was suffering from what Michael had told him. He wanted to see Rob happy again, and he knew Lola was the cure. Tony agreed to fly Rob to Boston and wait to bring them both back to Lewiston.

The flight was a little under two hours, and in that time, Rob felt himself grow increasingly nervous. What if she never wanted to see him again? What if it was too late? He knew she wouldn't be looking for anyone else, but what if someone else had found her? He bounced his leg up and down to release some of his nervous energy. She could always say no. She could tell him he was too late. What if she said no? What if it was too late?

All of the sudden a full-on, dimple-showing smile curved his lips. He was thinking of how she responded to his touch in the kitchen. How she totally abandoned all inhibitions to be with him. Unconsciously, he parted his lips, remembering the feel of her luscious lips upon his. He had shared his deepest, darkest secrets with her, and she had shared hers with him. That had to count for something.

Michael was right, she never left his side while he was in the hospital. Her blue eyes were like two priceless sapphires shining brightly at his when he woke up.

All Rob could feel was the emptiness that plagued his stomach. He wouldn't be whole again until she agreed to be his officially. Until she wore his ring.

How was he going to do it? He had to make it special. He had to make it so she couldn't possibly say no. He thought on the plan for the remainder of the flight.

Tony's voice announcing their approach to Boston brought him from his thoughts. As soon as he touched down, he was going to race to her brownstone and not leave until she agreed to see him. How long would he be kept outside waiting?

He was dressed in a nice button-down shirt with a nice pair of khaki cargo shorts. He had shaved the stubble from his face and thought he looked the best he could. He could only hope his genuine smile at seeing her was enough to gain him access to her home.

He had a new appreciation for the world, a new appreciation for life. He never knew life could be this sweet. He was up to his heart in love with Lola. He had to convince her. He had no other choice. A life without Lola wasn't a life.

The airplane touched down onto the runway. His hands trembled with impatience as he waited for the plane to taxi to the hub. Once at the hub, the ground workers wheeled the staircase over to the plane. Tony walked out to wish Rob good luck.

Rob took Tony's hand and pulled him in for a hug.

"You really think she loves me?" Rob asked, hope filling his light gray eyes.

"I know she does," Tony reassured his friend.

"Then I am going to get her and bring her back.

He got out of the rental SUV and stared at her brownstone. All of the 'what if's' were troubling his mind. But this time, it wasn't whether or not he wanted a child; this time it was whether or not Lola still wanted him.

He mustered his courage and walked slowly to her outer door. He raised his hand to knock but pulled back. Maybe this was a bad idea. Maybe he shouldn't ask her to marry him. He stared with an unfocused gaze at her door. He exhaled a shallow sigh. He closed his eyes to clearly recall the way she looked when he suggested she had options. The look of pure devastation in her eyes broke his heart all over again.

Butterflies took flight in his stomach as he warred with himself. He knew in that moment, whether or not she wanted him, he had to try. He wouldn't know until he did. He closed his eyes, his hands in his pockets as he tried to muster the courage to knock. Just then he felt wind pull against his face. He opened his eyes to a wide-eyed Lola. She stood there, mouth gaping open, eyes wide in shock.

She mumbled, "What are you doing here?"

"May I come in?" he cajoled.

"I was on my way out. I am meeting Jessica at the mall."

"Please. I need to talk to you. Please, Lola," Rob begged.

He was begging her to talk to him. That could only mean one thing, but she didn't want to get her hopes up. The last week had been the worst of her life. She felt lost and hopeless without Rob. When he rejected the baby and her, she gave up on living. Jessica had threatened bodily harm to get her out with her today.

"I'm sorry, Rob, but I have to meet Jessica," she whispered, hanging her head.

"I'm not leaving here until we can talk, Lola."

"If you're here when I get back, I'll talk with you." She had to get away from him. She had to clear her mind and think. He had devastated her. Was she making a mistake by leaving? She meant what she said, if he waited for her, then she would know he was serious. She pushed past him to her car parked in front of her brownstone. She got in the front seat and felt

278

extreme guilt for leaving him. After all, he did travel to get here. Too bad. If he wanted her, he would wait for her. That was her test for him. Although, she didn't need to tell him that. As she glanced over in his direction, she saw his body turn to sit upon the brownstone steps. Hope fluttered in her chest. Was he really going to wait for her?

She met Jessica at the open air, upscale mall. Jessica had hoped shopping for baby clothes would make Lola feel better. Jessica had been denied Lola's presence until today. Lola didn't want anybody but Rob. Jessica waved upon seeing Lola enter the square, and Lola quickly rushed to her side. "Rob is at my house."

"What? Wait. What?" Jessica asked, confused. "Why is he there?"

"He begged me to talk to him."

"And you left him? Are you crazy?"

"I had to get away from him. I had to talk to you. I don't know what he wants. But from the look in his eyes, I think he is here to apologize to me."

"Oh, hell no. He doesn't get to come in and say 'I'm sorry' and win your forgiveness that easy," Jessica counseled.

"That's what I thought, which is why I left him there to come meet you. I told him if he is there waiting when I return, then I would talk to him," Lola confided.

"What are you going to say to him? He rejected the baby."

"I didn't give him a chance to explain himself. I heard 'options' and automatically assumed the worst. I owe him the chance to explain. I'm in love with him, Jessica."

"I would make him work for it. I know you're in love with him. And hell, I even believe he is in love with you. What else would bring him here?" Jessica questioned.

"Maybe he wants to convince me to have an abortion? What if that is why he wants to talk to me?" Lola worried her bottom lip with her thumb and forefinger.

"Then you kick his ass out. That's your home."

"He saved my life twice, Jessica. He said he wanted to own me. He wanted me to be his. He couldn't have changed his mind that quickly," Lola said more to herself than to Jessica. Hope fluttered awake in her heart.

"What are you smiling at?" Jessica questioned, her head cocked to the side, trying to understand her friend.

"I'm just remembering lying in bed and talking with him. I'm remembering the way he said I belonged to him. I remember the way he said he would be the only man to have me as he caressed my body." Lola smiled, recalling the tender memories. "I am so in love with him, Jessica," she said to her best friend as she rose to her feet. Turning to face her friend, she said, "I have to hear what he has to say. I'm sorry. Will you take a raincheck for today?"

"Of course I will. Make him work for it. Don't give in too easily," Jessica laughed, calling after her friend who was now running out of the exit.

Lola pulled into her parking spot and nervously looked to her side to the steps to see if he still waited. Her heart dropped into her stomach when she saw he was gone. She lowered her chin to her chest as she got out of the car. She stumbled through her tears as she made her way to the stairs. Tears fell again uncontrollably at the thought of him leaving her a second time. She dug through her purse to find her key. With trembling hands, she finally found it and managed to get it in the deadbolt.

STRONGER

CHAPTER
THIRTY-FIVE

She felt a hand on her arm. She jerked and turned to stare wide-eyed at the man who stood before her with a bouquet of flowers in his hand.

Rob looked at the tears streaming down her face and knew in that instant she didn't need flowers; she needed him.

"I wanted to get these for you," he whispered, handing her the flowers. She smiled slowly at him, still afraid to let her walls down. But he had a way of wiggling into her defense system.

The site of his unshed tears made her cry more. He lifted his empty hands to her face. He brushed the tears from her cheeks with his thumb. Then, thinking he overstepped his bounds, he jerked his hands back at the energy that zinged through his body at the touch of her skin, like he had been electrocuted.

"Please let me talk to you, love," he begged.

She turned back to the door and silently unlocked it. She walked to the second set of doors without a word, still unsure if she could trust him again. But if she didn't give him this chance, she would always regret it. She walked through the door and left it open for him to enter.

He took the open door as his signal to follow her. He wasn't giving her a chance to turn him down. Walking quickly through the first door, he clicked it shut and locked it behind him. He entered into her living room, locking the second door as well. Then he stood there, unsure of how to proceed.

"Would you like something to drink?" she asked to break the awkward silence that stretched out between them.

"Water would be great, thank you," he responded.

She moved to the kitchen, pulled down two glasses from the cupboard, and filled them with ice and water. She returned to him in the living room. He was rooted to the same spot he took when he entered her home. She motioned towards the couch for him to sit down. She placed his water on the far end of the coffee table indicating his spot on the couch. She sat on the opposite end of the couch, uncomfortable with the tension which grew between them.

"Why are you here?" she exhaled on a breath she didn't realized she was holding.

"I need to explain a few things."

"I'm listening." She wasn't going to make this easy for him. If he wanted her forgiveness, he would have to work for it.

"When you first told me you were pregnant, I reacted out of fear."

"You think I'm not afraid?" she questioned.

"Please, Lola, let me finish. This is hard to admit to you. I don't want you to see me as less than a man."

"I could never think that of you," she confessed.

Hope bloomed in his chest at her admission. He continued. "You have to understand, I have given having children a great deal of thought when I was with Lizzie. And the same fears that plagued my mind with her came rushing back to me. Lots of 'what if' questions. What if someone used my child against me in a mission? What if my child was put into danger because of my job? I can't quit my job; it's all I know; it's who I am."

She started to speak, but he held up his hand, indicating for her to let him finish. "I was constantly thinking 'what if something happened to my child?' You have to know that I would kill anyone that tried to harm you or our baby."

She whipped her head up to look at him. "Our baby?"

"Michael came to talk to me the other night and made me see that my fears were irrational. He asked me one 'what if' question that the answer to is not something I can live with. It blew all of my worries and fears out of the water."

"What was the question?" she asked, hoping upon hope that he said the right thing.

"He asked what if you found someone else to love and that person wanted to raise my child?"

She exhaled a deep breath. "What are you saying, Rob?" She had to hear the words form on his lips before she could let down her defenses. She had to hear him say it before she could forgive him.

"I want you, Lola. I want us. I want this baby," he said. She looked at him with love and compassion filling her heart. He said it.

She moved closer to him on the couch, pulled her feet underneath her, and turned to face him so her knees were brushing against his leg. She felt the familiar energy radiate down her spine to her core. She felt the tingle spread over her body from the tips of her toes all the way to the top of her head.

She held his face with both her hands, and this time it was her that gently brushed the tear from his cheek. She leaned in until she was an inch away from his lips. She whispered, "I want that, too."

No sooner were the words out of her mouth then were his lips pressed passionately against hers. How he ever let her walk out of his life, he would never know. She deepened the kiss by searching out his tongue with hers. He pushed her back gently to lie on the couch. He unbuttoned her shirt and let it lie to the side of her body. Her pink lacy bra was affecting him. She was affecting him. He was straining against the zipper on his shorts. He unbuttoned her pants, and she lifted her hips, helping him remove them from her body. He admired her matching lacy panties for a moment before reaching to rid her of them as well. When she was naked from the waist down, he pulled his shirt over his head. She stared at his body. Each look a caress he felt to his core.

Lola watched as he removed his shorts and boxer briefs. He smiled that panty-dropping, two-dimple smile and said, "I guess we don't need a condom."

She smiled a heartfelt smile back at him. He nudged her legs open with his. He had to be inside her. Now. There should have been foreplay. He should have made sure she got off, but he could do nothing but enter her. He positioned himself at her opening. He pushed his tip inside her body and slowly buried himself to the hilt. She pulled his head until his lips met hers. He swallowed the moan that escaped her lips as he made love to her with his mouth, his body, his heart, his soul. He withdrew slowly and pushed back in again, which forced another moan from her lips. He continued his slow rhythm in and out until she found herself meeting his slow thrusts. She had her legs spread open, one leg lying against his calf, her other leg pressed against the back of the couch. He continued to make sweet love to her. He felt her spasms and knew she was close.

"Come with me. Look at me and come with me," he whispered into her ear, sending goose bumps down her entire body.

Never had she felt so thoroughly loved. No one had ever loved her like Rob. She looked into his eyes, seeing nothing but love reflected back to her. She knew in that moment that even if he never said it, he loved her. He did own her in that moment. He owned her heart. No one would ever have it but him. As she came, she kept eye contact with him, communicating the love she had refused to tell him. His body tensed and he came with her. Together they expanded out into the universe lifting from their bodies. They were truly united as one being as they floated back down from euphoria. He lay on top of her, staying buried inside her, kissing her for an eternity. He couldn't get enough of her sweet mouth.

He still had a question to ask her. After the love she made with him, he felt pretty confident in asking her, still an uncertainty reared its ugly head. He stood. "Stay here. I'll clean you up."

He ran to the upstairs bathroom and retrieved a washcloth. He wet it, rang it out, and returned to where she laid unmoving, enjoying the feeling of bliss that now filled her body. She had her Rob back. He wanted a family, with her. She still couldn't believe her dreams were coming true.

He cleaned her gently between her legs, taking care over the sensitive nub of her body.

"Are you hungry? I can make us something to eat," she asked with a genuine smile playing on her lips.

Rob couldn't believe he had the power to make someone so deliriously happy. He enjoyed the feeling. "We can cook together. Besides, I'm going to take care of you from here on out."

"Rob, I'm not sick. I'm pregnant. I can still cook. Besides, I want to cook for my man," she cooed.

He held his hands up in surrender. "I will eat anything my love decides to cook." That was the closest he came to telling her how he felt. He still had that and one more hurdle to cross.

She got dressed and made her way to the kitchen. He stayed on the couch where they just made love for the first time and collected his courage.

All of his irrational fears came flooding back to him. He tried to calm his nerves by remembering Michael's question. *"What would life be like without her?"*

That question made him stop biting his bottom lip. He stood and stalked to the kitchen. It was now or never. She had her back to him and didn't see him get down on one knee. She turned to get an ingredient and jumped when his presence startled her.

Quickly her hands started to tremble. She jerked and spilled the ingredients all over him. He stayed true, not moving. He reached for her hands. Taking both hands in hers, he looked up at her through thick, black lashes, meeting her sparkling blue eyes. He could hear his heart beating their love in his ears.

"Lola. I…I'm in love with you. I know you probably think this is too fast, but when you know it's right, you know. And I know, Lola. I can't and won't imagine a life where you are not mine. I want you to tell me you're mine by wearing this ring." He opened the box, and her eyes found the stunning one carat diamond engagement ring. Tears streamed down her face and fell against their joined hands. "Lola, will you do me the honor and say that you will be mine forever? Will you marry me?"

He barely got "me" out of his mouth and she was on her knees in front of him. She took his face in her hands and asked one simple question. "Why?"

"Because I can't and won't imagine a life where you don't belong to me. You are carrying my child. I want our child with you Lola as much as I want my next breath. I want the family, the white picket fence, and as many rug rats as you want running around causing us chaos and sleepless nights. Because I know, no matter what we go through, we will go through it together, as a team. You will be mine. But equally, I will be yours. For better or worse, Lola.

A sob racked her body as warmth radiated through her entire being. She threw her arms around his neck. "Yes," she whispered.

He pulled her back with wide eyes. Did he hear her right? He believed he did and was going with it. He slid the ring onto her ring finger. As he did, she said, "I am so in love with you, Rob Fabik."

He leaned in and kissed her with more passion, more fire, more desire, more love than he had ever known could exist. She was his, and now the world would know.

"You have made me the happiest man alive. Together, we will be stronger than ever. I love you, Lola."

The End

SARAH GREYSON

I want to hear from you. To contact me, follow one of the following links.

Email: Sarah@SarahGreyson.com
Website: https://www.sarahgreyson.com
Amazon Author page: http://www.amazon.com/-/e/B00L99CNY2
aboutme: http://about.me/sarahgreyson
Google+: http://bit.ly/GooglePlusSarahGreyson
Twitter: https://twitter.com/Sarah_G_Greyson
Facebook: http://bit.ly/SarahGreysonsFacebookPage
Pinterest: http://www.pinterest.com/Greysonnovels/
Tumblr: http://sarahgreyson.tumblr.com/